FAT

Labels #1

By Saranna DeWylde

All rights reserved. No part of this publication may be reproduced, stored in a retrieval system, or transmitted in any form or by any means (electronic, mechanical, photocopying, recording, or otherwise) without the prior written permission of both the copyright owner and the publisher. The only exception is brief quotations in printed reviews.

The scanning, uploading, and distribution of this book via the Internet or via any other means without the permission of the publisher is illegal and punishable by law. Please purchase only authorized electronic editions, and do not participate in or encourage electronic piracy of copyrighted materials. Your support of the author's rights is appreciated. If you downloaded this illegally, please consider buying your own copy. Or at least leave a review.

Published in the United States of America by Saranna DeWylde

© 2014 Saranna DeWylde

Cover Art Design by Saranna DeWylde
Stockphoto by Dreamstime

ISBN-13:
978-1497471757

ISBN-10:
1497471753

FAT

By Saranna DeWylde

FAT

CHAPTER ONE

"You're pretty. For a fat girl."

For a second, I wasn't sure it had actually happened. An insult is one thing, but that kind of "compliment" is like getting hit in the face with a baseball. You feel the impact, but then you go numb and you're never quite sure if something's broken or not.

But no blood gushed down my face and when my vision cleared from the cloud of disbelief, I could see none running down his face either. He didn't know it, but today was his lucky day. It was even money whether I would have punched him or not.

I took a deep breath, and smiled. "You're hot. For a douchebag."

I decided that since I'd done the time, I might as well do the crime and headed over to the dessert table. Champagne and chocolate truffle cheesecake for my trouble.

"Oh, hey. Come on. I didn't mean it like that," he said, as he walked up behind me.

I've never understood this about people. What other way could he possibly mean it? It wasn't that I thought "fat" was an insult. It was an adjective, like any other. No, it was the way he said it that was insulting. The compliment that came with a condition, the kiss before the kick. It seemed to me like fatness had become the last legal and socially acceptable form of discrimination. Like anyone could just say anything to me, because I dared to exist while being fat.

"You know what you look like," he said.

I didn't even know this guy's name and I had to say that I didn't care to. "Are you talking to me? And if so, *why* are you still talking to me?" And I *did* know what I looked like. I was 5'10 and a size twenty-six, with DDD breasts that looked *amazing* in my cherry-print pin-up dress, which complemented my victory-rolled hair, my half-sleeve of tattoos and my Kat Von D lipstick in *Oh My Goth*. Yeah, I knew what I looked like. I looked fucking fabulous.

"Because you're pretty."

"For a fat girl," I added. "There, I fixed that for you."

"Okay, so maybe that didn't come out the way I meant it."

"I'm pretty sure it did." I grabbed a flute of champagne and scanned the crowd for April. It was her birthday and she was the only reason I'd bothered to show up to a party at—I looked around for the name of the restaurant—somewhere I couldn't pronounce, let alone afford.

"Look, I was just startled. I've never been attracted to a woman like you before."

"I've never been attracted to a man like you." That was a lie. I'd spent my teen years pining over guys like him. Perfect smile, broad shoulders, chiseled jaw… the standard football player-boy-next-door type who only went for size zero, blond, cheerleaders. I had no reason to set myself up for that kind of disappointment.

"Can we start over? I'm Gavin."

I finally turned to look at him. He seemed sincere. I'd done my own share of tripping over my tongue and I guess the least I could do was agree. That didn't mean I had to like him, or talk to him, or even go home with him. It was just a conversation. I'd taught myself a long time ago not to let words mean anything to me. Unless they were my own.

"I'm Claire."

"I know." He looked sheepish. "April and I work together at Bausch."

Oh sweet Jesus. This was *the* Gavin she was always talking about wanting to set me up with. "Well, I guess that was a big fail, wasn't it?"

"What was?" He cocked his head to the side.

Heat climbed my neck and spread up over my face. I was sure I was blushing. She must not have mentioned it to him. Color me embarrassed. "Nothing. I've got to go."

"You just got here."

"Seems that way, doesn't it?" I started scanning the crowd for my roommate, Kieran. He'd driven us there, since my car was currently in the garage and would probably be there until shit stuck to the moon, or I paid off my Torrid credit card. Neither would ever happen.

"Can I give you my card?"

"Why would you want to do that?"

"You make it hard on a guy. I'm trying to ask you out."

I knew his type. He thought since I was fat, I was easy. He'd show me a little attention, I wouldn't say no because guys like him didn't like girls like me. What a bunch of crap. Before I could answer, it was as if Kieran had sensed my distress and was at my side. He was a great wingman.

"You ready to go? We've got that thing." He nodded to the door.

"Yeah. Let me find April and say goodbye."

"She's coming to the thing." He grabbed my elbow.

Wait, there was actually a thing? I raised a brow.

He grinned. "It's her birthday. Did you really think the guys weren't going to do something for her? Come on. I've got to get changed."

What he meant was he had to get naked. Kieran was an exotic dancer at a ladies club called The Rooster.

"What's the thing?" Gavin asked, following us.

I stopped and turned to look at him. "Male strippers. Want to come?"

It was my turn to throw the baseball that hit him in the face, but he recovered quickly. "If you'll give me your number after."

Kieran grinned. "Sorry, laddie. Not unless you want to clamber up on stage and give it a shot." His Irish accent was a bit more pronounced.

And that was why I loved Kieran. He was always up for any scheme or adventure.

"Why not?" Gavin shrugged.

Why not, indeed.

Kieran laughed. "Meet us there. It's The Rooster, over off of 119th."

"Even money he doesn't show," Kieran said after we were in his shiny, black Dodge Challenger.

"I hope he doesn't. That's the guy April kept trying to set me up with."

"Well, is that the only thing that's wrong with him—that April wanted to set you up?"

"No, that's not the problem. He said I was pretty. For a fat girl."

"Did you junk-punch him?"

"No. But he seemed determined to want to hook up for some reason."

He nodded to my ample cleavage. "Yeah, *some* reason."

"Shut up." I laughed it off and poked through his iPod and put ZZ Ward on.

"I forgot to delete that from my playlist. Jesus, woman. If you played her anymore, you would *be* her."

The woman was gorgeous and could wail her heart out. "There are worse things to be."

"Yeah, like stuck in a car with you while you angst over her lyrics."

"I am not angsting."

"Yeah? Prove it."

"How's that?"

"Go out with Brant."

"Nope." Brant was another guy who worked at the club. "I just can't do it."

"So you wanted Douchie McDickface earlier to see you for more than your body, but you're guilty of the same thing. Tell me there's any other reason that you won't go out with him than he's 5'6."

I bit my lip. He was right. "We can't help who we're attracted to." I held up my hand to stop him from pouncing on that. "But, I never told Brant I wouldn't go out with him because he was 5'6. I didn't say 'you're hot for a midget.' Because I'm not an asshole."

"But you thought it and that kind of makes you an asshole, too."

Ugh. He was right. I slumped in the seat.

"He really likes you."

"It's not just that he's short. I could never date someone who does what you guys do. I'm not wired that way. I have a hard enough time keeping my confidence up without worrying about every pretty girl with a fantasy and a credit card."

"But you know that's all it is, right? A fantasy? I'm just Kieran when I'm not at the club."

I rolled my eyes. "So says you who has a parade of pussy through our house."

He smirked. "I'd do that even if I didn't dance."

"I'm probably the only woman in the city you haven't banged."

Kieran looked thoughtful for a moment. "No, I haven't banged April, but she kind of wanted that for her birthday present."

I couldn't tell if he was kidding or not. "You're such a slut."

He shrugged. "If the G-string fits."

"Why didn't you tell me about the trip to The Rooster?" I changed the subject. I wouldn't have worn the cherry dress because now it was going to forever smell like man-musk and that glitter oil they used. It wasn't a bad smell, in fact, I kind of liked it. I just didn't want my cherry dress to smell that way for now and always.

"Because I knew you'd try to find some way out of it. Now, I've got you in the car and there is no escape."

"Is there ever?" I sighed dramatically. Not that it was actually a chore to go to The Rooster, but I think I would have enjoyed it more if I didn't know most of the guys outside the club. They came to our house, they helped me move big furniture, and worked on my car. Sometimes, I'd babysit their kids. It seemed decidedly wrong to objectify a man after I'd taken his daughter to the zoo and she now called me Auntie Claire.

"When was the last time you actually had any fun?"

I bit my lip again. I hated how well he knew me. "I've been working pretty hard on the website and the dress designs for *Chubbalicious*. The launch is in two weeks. If everything isn't perfect, I don't know what I'm going to do. My degree will be for nothing and I'll be out of funding. I'll worry about having fun after I have a steady paycheck."

Kieran shook his head. "I can't imagine living the nine to five like that. Sounds like misery."

"Not at all. I'm doing exactly what I want to do. And I'm working way more than nine to five."

"Right, you're working, but you're not living."

"I'll live when I can afford to live."

"No one can ever afford to live. I came to the States with barely a hundred euro and the clothes on my back."

"You're also slightly insane." The idea of just flinging myself to the wind like that and rolling with wherever I landed was terrifying. I couldn't imagine just deciding I was sick of a place, throwing a dart at a map, and moving.

"You love me anyway."

"Don't let it go to your head." I did love him. For all of his craziness, I could always depend on Kieran. In fact, if *Chubbalicious* failed miserably, Kieran would cover me until I got on my feet. I didn't want to need that safety net, but it was nice to know it was there.

"Never that, lass." He winked at me.

"Don't start being cute."

"I never stopped."

I rolled my eyes. That was really the only thing I could do when faced with his Irish charm. Sarcasm was a kind of armor I used to shield myself. Because as much as I did love Kieran, it would be beyond stupid for me to have any feelings for him other than friendship. When he played up that lilting accent, coupled with his genuine grin and handsome face, it was my only defense.

"I still think you should go out with Brant."

"So noted." I narrowed my eyes at him. "Why are you suddenly a Brant fanboy?"

He didn't look at me. Of course, he was driving, but it seemed like he was avoiding meeting my eyes. "I just feel bad for him, and you need to have some fun."

"Fine. If it'll make you stop poking me about it, I'll go."

He finally looked at me. "If I was poking you, you'd know it."

I rolled my eyes again. "I have no desire to be number three hundred in a series of a thousand."

"You give me too much credit."

I eyed him and then he grinned again.

"Okay, that was a lie. But you know I love you, Claire-Bear."

He pulled in to the parking lot of The Rooster.

It was a plain, refurbished warehouse without much to recommend it on the outside. A giant chicken had been freshly painted on to the side of the brick building and it made me giggle.

"Yes, that's a giant cock." Kieran added helpfully.

"Actually, it's not." That made me laugh harder. "It's a hen."

"Only you would notice that." He shook his head. "Remember, you agreed to talk to Brant."

"As if I could forget."

April pulled up in the car next to us with Gavin, Hollie and Rosa.

This was going to make for an interesting night. I stole another glance at Kieran and wondered if he was really going to sleep with April.

He got out and went around to her car to open the door for her.

Yeah, he was totally going to hit that.

I sighed.

This wasn't going to end well. In the beginning, I asked that my friends be off limits. I know that was selfish and totally not my decision, but if he was going to use them like Shake N' Bake bags, I'd be the one to listen to them cry about it when he didn't call.

April acted like this was just a hook up, but she'd had a thing for Kieran for years.

Gavin opened the door for me. "You can't stay in the car, you know."

"Why not?"

"Because it's April's birthday."

"She wants to bang Kieran, not me." I smirked. "She won't notice."

"She will definitely notice. Come on. I'll buy you a cranberry vodka."

"Now you're speaking my language." One drink wouldn't hurt. Plus, I'd agreed to a date with Brant. If he asked. If I was sitting with Gavin, he might not ask.

It wasn't that Brant was a bad guy, I knew Kieran wouldn't push me toward anyone who was an asshole. But it was like I said earlier, I couldn't handle dating a guy who stripped for a living.

Logically, I knew that people chose their own actions. Simply by virtue of being an exotic dancer didn't mean he was going to cheat on me, but I saw how Kieran was. And I knew that there were women of all shapes and sizes that came through The Rooster and I just didn't want to sign up for that kind of angst. Especially not when I had a business to get off the ground.

And let's face it: Brant was 5'6. But that wasn't any kind of failing on his part. I knew that. It was a failing on my part that I wasn't confident enough to be seen with a man that much smaller than me and not feel like Moby freaking Dick.

That was the part I couldn't confess to Kieran. I had him fooled, I had most of them fooled. There were days I even had myself fooled and I believed everything I said about thinking I was beautiful and sexy at any size.

When I'd first gotten to the party, I'd felt great about myself.

Until Gavin.

I'd really like it if some day, some guy would just tell me I'm beautiful. I'm not beautiful for my size, beautiful for a fat girl, or that I have a "beautiful face" implying that the rest of it wasn't worth anyone's time.

I'd really just like to be beautiful.

And Kieran telling me didn't count. He was my friend. He was supposed to say that. Not to mention he was the Manwhore of LaMancha. He could find something beautiful about any woman.

I wanted to be special.

I kind of thought Brant's interest was more to just be able to say he'd climbed the mountain. Either that or because the first time he asked, I'd said no. I'd taken enough marketing classes to know that people always wanted what they couldn't have.

Gavin brought me the vodka and cranberry, but Kieran barely let him set it down on our table before he pounced.

"I wasn't kidding, boy-o. You wanted to come in, you've got to dance. You're going up first since you're the newb."

Gavin grinned. "Whatever, man. How do you think I paid for my MB?"

Really? I wondered if April knew this.

"Stage name is Adonis." Gavin winked at me and allowed Kieran to lead him backstage.

April was immediately in the chair next to me. "So? Do you like him?"

I was in hell. "We're not a good fit."

April flopped back in her chair. "You say that about everyone."

"Because it's true about everyone." I took a drink of my vodka and cranberry. "But why are you even worried about me tonight? It's your birthday." I debated mentioning anything about Kieran, but as usual, my tongue did what it wanted before my brain could say yea or nay. "I hear you're getting a special present from Kieran."

April pursed her lips and blushed. "I know you don't approve, but—"

Approve? When had I become everyone's mom? *Ugh.* "It's not that I don't approve, I just don't want you to get hurt."

"It's just a little sex, right? He's the fantasy." April shrugged. "I'm going to have a night with Finn McCool, not Kieran. I *do* know there's a difference."

There was so much I wanted to say to her, but I realized it all sounded judgmental which would accomplish exactly nothing. She'd made up her mind. "Okay."

"Okay? That's it?"

"What else am I going to say? Have fun and don't be that chick who won't go home."

"Bitch." She elbowed me lightly.

We made fun of those women that Kieran brought home and who wouldn't leave, or who kept calling long after he was done with them. Especially the ones who were jealous of me. That was especially funny. They were the ones who didn't understand that Finn was a character and Kieran was real.

The seat on the other side of me was suddenly occupied.

"Hey, gorgeous." Brant smiled. "You want another drink?"

"No, I'm good. Thanks."

April leaned around my shoulder. "She's here with Gavin."

Brant snorted. "That guy? Not a chance."

I couldn't help the grin that bloomed on my face. "He said I was pretty for a fat girl."

"He what?" April's face darkened to a thundercloud.

"It's not a big deal. I told him he was hot for a douchebag. We're all good." Except there was still this strange hollow feeling in my chest.

"With a stage name like Adonis? He's got douchebag written all over him." Brant smiled at me. It *was* a nice smile. "I'll put Icy Hot on his G-string."

Laughing, I said, "No. There's no need for that. Frankly, when Kieran told him he had to dance if he wanted to come with us, I thought that was punishment enough."

"Are you here with him?" Brant asked quietly.

"No."

"So maybe you'll leave with me? We'll grab breakfast."

I remembered my promise to Kieran and maybe he was right. Brant had never told me I was pretty for a fat girl. He told me I was gorgeous—without any caveats—all the time. He'd asked me out a dozen times, I'd always said no, but he always kept asking.

"Okay." I hoped I wouldn't regret it.

"Great. I'll see you after the show." He brushed a kiss against my cheek. That wasn't any unusual behavior, they all kissed my cheek. And April's, and Hollie's, and Rosa's and…

"What was that?" April asked when he'd gone.

The lights came down and a waiter brought us more drinks, and presented April with a birthday tiara which she allowed him to affix on her head.

"I promised Kieran I'd give Brant a chance."

"Well, look at you. I guess you do find the good ones on your own. I still can't believe Gavin said that to you. I swear, he's never been that kind of douche in all the years I've known him."

"He tried to make it up to me. I mean, he's here. Don't hold it against him." I remembered my earlier conversation with Kieran again. "He can't help who he's attracted to or not. No one can."

"Yeah, but it's not like you're one of those girls. You know who I mean. The kind who doesn't take care of themselves. You're pretty, smart, witty, kind… and your boobs… girl, I kind of hate you for them."

I'd always thought that was my one saving grace. My giant breasts. I was lucky because even if I somehow managed to lose the weight, I'd still have boobs. It wasn't like they were just another roll I'd stuffed into a bra. They were shapely, bouncy, and I had magnificent cleavage.

As to losing the weight, I'd tried. I still tried. I did yoga, cardio, and weight training. I watched what I ate, counted calories… But having endocrine and autoimmune issues, I'd just kind of given up that my body would ever look the way I wanted.

At least I had my breasts. And if a woman who looked like April was jealous of them, well, that was saying something. She was traditionally beautiful. If I had to describe her using an actress, I'd say Kate Beckinsale. Who can compete with that? The bitch of it was, she was nice too. April was the whole package.

I tried to remind myself that I was the whole package too. I really hated feeling this way. I needed to go home and reread some Militant Baker blog posts. My favorite one was about the things no one tells fat girls. It always made me feel better after reading it. It had become a kind of mantra.

"Are you doing that thing in your head again?" April asked me.

"No." I turned to look at her. "Yes." She knew me too well. It was why she was one of my best friends.

"Stop it."

"I know." I shrugged. "Consider me done with it. *I'm fabulous. You're fabulous.* It's your birthday and you have a date with Finn McCool."

"I do, don't I?" April exhaled heavily. "Am I crazy?"

"No." Actually, I admired her. She saw something she wanted and she reached out and took it. I wished I was that kind of woman. "You're a total badass."

"But I'm really not sure how I'll ever look Gavin in the face again. This is either going to be really awful or really good."

"Just think of it as blackmail material."

"Who are we blackmailing?" Hollie piped up as she scooted closer to us.

"Gavin Woodlawn," April answered.

"Oh, really? I'd love to get a bite of him."

"He's here for Claire," April said.

"Well, who isn't? Claire gets everyone."

I turned my head sharply. "What do you mean?"

"You live with Kieran, Brant wants to go out with you and now Gavin is here just to hang out with you. You need to share some of that booty with the rest of us."

"You want half?" I sat straight up in my seat and nodded to my backside.

"I've got plenty of *that* booty myself. You know I meant your harem of beefcake."

"Brant just asked me on one date, Gavin is here to make up for something crappy he said, and Kieran and I are just friends."

"Please," Hollie said, holding up her hand. "You can't tell me that you haven't thought about just stumbling into the shower while Kieran's in there. Oops, sorry, I didn't know you were in here and oh look, we're both naked." Then she pantomimed thrusting with her hips.

"It looks like there's more of a show down here at table three than anything on stage. How about it, pretty lady? Want to try your hand or your hips on stage tonight?" the MC said and shined a light on our table.

Hollie wasn't about to be outdone. "Hell yeah. I owe this birthday girl a lap dance!" She motioned to April and shimmied to rub her boobs against the back of her head.

"I think that's something we'd all like to see. But for now, how about all the hens get ready to watch the cocks strut the yard?"

A cheer went up and the spotlight was back on the stage as the curtain slowly revealed our entertainment for the evening.

I tried not to look at Kieran. He wasn't Kieran now, he was Finn McCool. He wasn't my friend, my roommate, he was a fantasy come to life. That's what they all were. Which should have made it okay for me to eye fuck him, but it was a trespass.

And twisted bitch that I was, that made me want to look at him even more. That's why he put himself on the stage, so it was okay to indulge, right?

When he winked at me, I realized I wasn't so different from any of the women here. In fact, I was screwed and not in a good way.

I wanted Kieran Holt.

CHAPTER TWO

I waited a reasonable amount of time before fleeing upstairs to the roof where the dancers took their breaks. I'd been at the club so often, it was almost like I worked there too. So no one said anything to me when I took the employee stairs.

The night was warm with a bit of a breeze. I wrapped my arms around myself as I sat on the picnic table and looked out over the city. I'd always loved this view. The bright city lights, the sounds, it was only the pretty things. The bright things. I didn't have to examine anything too closely, I could just experience it.

In fact, the top of The Rooster was one of my favorite places.

I inhaled deeply and tried to avoid thinking about what made me run here to start with.

Except now that I'd acknowledged it, I couldn't think about anything but how much I wanted Kieran.

It was a physical ache.

How pathetic was that?

He was sleeping with one of my best friends as a birthday gift. A guy who thought about physicality in those terms certainly wasn't the guy for me. Only my heart didn't want to listen.

The treacherous bitch.

Everything clicked into place. Kieran was why I hadn't dated anyone in a year. It was both cathartic and painful to realize the truth of it.

I guessed GI Joe was right, knowing really was half the battle. I needed to get him out of my head. It was okay to be his friend, it was okay to think he was handsome or even hot, it was quite another to want to be with him.

One guy said something crappy to me tonight and it wound me up for hours, what would it be like dating Kieran? They'd all wonder if I was his sugar mama, if I was paying his bills, or what exactly I had over him that might explain why a guy like him would ever date a woman like me.

A fat woman.

I closed my eyes. Shit. I wasn't supposed to feel this way. I thought I was done with that. I was confident. I was beautiful. I was powerful.

I repeated these things over and over to myself until I believed them. Or so I thought.

The woman I wanted to be, if she decided she wanted to be with Kieran, she'd make that happen. But instead, the woman I was just wanted to cauterize it. Cut it out like a cancer.

Part of me wanted to go back downstairs and swill vodka until I didn't feel this way anymore. When my face started to go numb, so would my feelings, and most importantly, my insecurities.

I liked to drown them. They had it coming. My liver would get over it.

I inhaled and looked back out over the city.

"Hey, you're missing Gavin's set," Rosa said from the door.

"Yeah, I'm okay with that."

She sat down next to me. "You know, I don't think he meant it how it sounded."

I shrugged. "That's over and done with. I really don't care about what he said or how he meant it. Really, I'm fine." It hurt, to be sure, but I had bigger things to worry about.

"Then why are you up here by yourself?"

"Just thinking about a new design for *Chubbalicious*." I used that to hide many sins. Whenever I was distracted, or just didn't want to deal with things, I could plead Chubbalicious.

"You have to stop working sometime."

"Why?"

"So you can do something that's fun?"

"Work is fun."

"You don't have to deal with people at work. You just have to tweak modules and play with the designs." Rosa admonished.

"So, you see why I feel like a puppy at a preschool? I'm definitely overstimulated."

Rosa smirked. "Overstimulated? At a strip club? Isn't that the point?"

I found myself smiling. "I'll be back down in a little bit."

"Promise? Because if you spend the whole night up here, April is going to be pissed."

"She wouldn't notice. She's got her Finn McCool thing going on." I waved her off. "But I promise, I'll be down soon."

"Don't make me come back up here and drag you down. If you do, I'm bringing reinforcements." Rosa went back through the door.

I leaned flat on the picnic table and looked up at the sky. That was something about the city that I didn't like so well. I couldn't see as many of the stars. It was important to me to see them, to feel wonder when I looked up at the sky. For some reason, it helped me breathe. It made me feel small and insignificant, but kind of magical at the same time.

"Don't you just look like a midnight picnic," Brant said from the door.

I sat up and smoothed my hands down the bodice and skirt of the dress. "I thought you were getting ready to go on."

"I've got more important business."

My smile came easy. "Really? Like what?"

"Like you." He was serious. "I've been asking you out forever and now that you finally said yes, I don't want you to change your mind."

"It's a little early for breakfast then, isn't it?" The club didn't close until two and he wouldn't get out of there until three, so late night truck stop breakfast was one of the only things to do.

"We can do whatever you want. Dinner. Late movie."

Whatever I wanted? My mind blanked. "It's been so long since I've been out with someone, I don't even know what we're supposed to do."

He shrugged. "Supposed to?" Brant made a face. "Fuck that. How about whatever we want to do?"

Suddenly, there wasn't so much pressure to be any certain thing. To do any certain thing. It was just spending time together. That was something that logically I knew, but my social anxiety tried to convince me otherwise.

I grabbed my phone and texted the girls. *Leaving with Brant. Catch you later. Xo*

April wouldn't care, but she'd want juicy details tomorrow morning. When she could walk. Hell, she'd probably be in my kitchen doing unspeakable things to my Keurig by the time I got up anyway.

After doing depraved things to my roommate. Damn it, I didn't want to think about that.

"So what do you want to do?" I asked.

"There's a late evening river cruise." He checked his watch. "We might just make it. Or we can do the carriage ride on the Plaza."

Those were much better options than the standard dinner and a movie gig. "The river cruise sounds fun. Are you sure you want to give up a Saturday night, though?" I knew the weekend was when they made the most money.

"I can afford a night off. My car's in the lot."

We took a seldom used exit to make our escape. He took my hand to help me down the stairs. His fingers were warm and strong curled around mine. Our hands were about the same size.

He was shorter than me by four inches, but he wasn't exactly small. He wasn't waif-like or slight. He had nice shoulders and guns just like all the guys that worked at The Rooster.

"Watch that last stair." He still held my hand and made sure I didn't trip. And all things being equal, I would have.

"Thanks."

We went out to his car, a classic '67 Shelby Mustang. Red. "I'm going to have to take over the parking lot of The Rooster when I do my fashion shoots for *Chubbalicious*. I want girls on all of these cars wearing my designs." I was only half teasing. That would make for an awesome spread.

"I'm game."

Inspiration struck. "Dude. I want you and Kieran and maybe a few other guys in the shoot, too."

"But you're not selling men's clothes."

"No, but I'm selling an idea. An idea that women can be sexy no matter their size. And who better to show that than you guys all posed with my models?"

"Are you going to be in the shoot?"

"Certainly not. I'm the designer. Not the model."

"I'll pose with *you*."

I laughed. That was crazy. I couldn't put myself in the campaign. Could I? More importantly, did I want to? I hated pictures of myself more than a double-barreled yeast infection. Even before I'd gotten fat, I hated pictures of me. That's not to say I didn't think I was pretty. I was. But I wasn't photogenic.

"How about one for you with me, and then you pose with Rosa for the site?"

"I guess I can work with that." He grinned. "So are all of your friends posing? April isn't exactly…"

I waited to see what word he was going to use.

"…*Chubbalicious*."

That was about as tactful as he could be. "No, she's not. She might model some of the shoes because she really wants to be involved."

"You can't say that doesn't feel good." He pulled out of the parking lot and headed toward the river.

"What?"

"Having something that's just for you. Something that her physicality keeps her from doing."

I wasn't sure how to respond. I'd admit, it made me happy in a way to be able to say that she was too thin for my line. If she'd put out a clothing line, I'd never even ask to model for her. But even that made me feel shitty.

"It's the same for me and Kieran," Brant confided before I could reply. "He and I have been friends for a long time. Did you know I bench as much as he does, but when he picks up a woman during his act none of them ever wonder if he's going to be able to hold them up."

"And they do with you?"

He flashed me a look that said I should know better. "You wouldn't let me pick you up."

"I wouldn't let Kieran pick me up either."

"Bullshit. I seem to recall Rosa's birthday when you got hammered and Kieran carried you to the car."

"And he bitched about his back the whole way."

"Only because he didn't want you to struggle and hurt yourself."

I pursed my lips. "He could have just said that."

"No, he couldn't have. You were determined to dance that night and you flung yourself off the pole and if he hadn't caught you…" He shrugged.

"What? I don't remember that." I would never get that drunk.

"Of course you don't. You were toasted." He grinned. "It was a good show, though. You can work that pole."

Heat suffused my face. "I don't know if I should take that as a compliment or not."

"From a stripper? Definitely a compliment. Didn't you wonder why you had all those dollar bills in your bra?"

"I didn't have any dollar bills."

Brant laughed. "I bet Kieran kept them. That asshole."

That meant Kieran had been foraging around in my bra like a squirrel. He'd had his hands on my breasts.

Oh Jesus, I couldn't think about that right now. I *shouldn't* think about that. I was out with Brant. Brant who was nice, Brant who thought I was beautiful. Brant who didn't fucking *live in my house*.

Change the subject, but don't be too obvious. "Is Brant your stage name?"

"No. I'm really just Brant Bowman."

"That sounds like a superhero name."

"Right? I didn't see the need to take a stage name." He snorted. "Adonis. Jesus. *That* guy."

"Yeah, I'm glad I didn't see his bit. Especially since he was just there trying to get my digits after being a colossal ass."

He slowed the Mustang to a stop in an almost empty lot. "Looks like this is going to be an interesting ride."

Brant paid for our fare and we boarded the boat. I only saw one other couple board after us and soon we cruised the river at a leisurely pace.

"So, are you okay being stuck with me alone for an hour and a half?"

It was strange—life. Before going to The Rooster, I thought being alone with him would be pretty damn horrible, but it wasn't. I thought it would be like being in a pressure cooker with all this expectation, but we were just hanging out.

"It's not what I expected, so yeah." Shit. That sounded bad.

"Oh really?" He laughed. "What did you expect?"

I shrugged. "I don't know. I'm not very good in social situations. I feel like I'm supposed to be this certain thing all the time."

"Didn't we just say fuck 'supposed to'?"

"Yeah." I nodded. "That's why I'm having fun."

The air on the river was a little chillier and I probably should've brought a sweater. I must have shivered because Brant grabbed me and before I realized it, he'd maneuvered me so I leaned back against his chest and we were half-reclined on the bench; his arms around me and his chin resting on the crown of my head.

He was so warm and he smelled so good, a light splash of D&G Blue. It was easy to forget he was a dancer, easy to forget that I'd been avoiding him for months, and easy to forget he was four inches shorter than me.

This felt good and nothing had felt good in a long time. It was nice to be touched. Held. Treasured.

I looked up at the stars again.

"You do that a lot."

"What?"

"Look up at the stars. That's what you were doing on the roof of The Rooster."

"It's one of my favorite things to do."

"Do you know the constellations?"

"Some of them, but they mostly look like flecks of glitter on velvet. No particular shape, so I can't really identify them by sight. Like, right there?" I pointed. "That's the Little Dipper. And that's all I've got."

His hands started moving up and down my bare arms slowly, his callused fingers slightly rough. My body responded, I was hyperaware of everything. The hitch in my breath, the breeze on my skin in the wake of his caress, the hard ridge digging into my hip.

It had been so long since I'd been with someone, I'd forgotten how good this part was—the chase. The build-up where every touch primed you for more. His thumbs brushed the edges of my breasts as he stroked—made me wonder what would happen if I turned into his hand.

Of course, here on a boat in the middle of the river wasn't exactly the right place to do that. This was the tease. I braced my hands on his thighs and they were solid as concrete. I repositioned myself, but really it was just an excuse to rub myself against him and offer the best view of my cleavage.

He grew bolder with his touch, dragging his fingers over my collar bone, down my arm, then back up again. It was a challenge not to arch my back, demand more. I wanted his hands all over me.

I'd already decided I was going to sleep with him, that was a given. This all felt much too good to deny myself.

"Your skin is so soft." He continued in the same, unhurried manner—as if he'd be content to pet me like some kitten all night.

It was time to up the ante. I'd tell him what I wanted. It was easy for me to do that when I already knew a guy wanted me. I knew all the tricks, all the moves... I played the game of seduction well. As long as it was a guaranteed win.

I flexed my fingers around his jean-clad thighs, lightly kneading. "And you're so hard."

"Yeah, I am." His breath was warm against my ear and his stroking stopped.

I made a small sound of protest, but one arm was around my waist while the other, the one that was between me and the back of the bench, moved so that his hand slid under my dress—hidden by my crinoline.

To any passerby, we just appeared to be a couple cuddling under the stars.

But my breath caught in my throat as his hand moved steadily up between my thighs.

"Do you want this, Claire?"

Who wouldn't? "Yes."

He was like some kind of magician, dipping his fingers past my panties and moving in a primal rhythm that lit me on fire.

"I'm going to make you come so hard and long you'll beg me to stop."

"Tell me how."

"You like it dirty?" he asked in a low tone.

Apparently, I did tonight. It was like I was possessed, I wasn't me. I wasn't this wanton thing, this woman who let a guy do these things to her in a public place. Or on a first date.

But I didn't want to be Claire anyway. I wanted to be the version of Claire I painted up like some goddess of womanhood and confidence. The version I always pretended to be.

"I like it dirty, I like it clean—I just like it."

"You're so wet and hot. I can't wait to taste you." He plunged deeper, his thumb brushing lightly over my clit.

Shivers of pleasure and anticipation ricocheted through me and I struggled not to buck my hips too obviously.

"You're so fucking beautiful."

The orgasm that hit me was unexpected and almost uncomfortable. There'd been no long, slow build. No ratcheting up of sensation, it just crashed into me like a wrecking ball. I just shuddered against his hand.

I knew what had done it, what had pushed me over the edge. His raw confession about how he thought I was beautiful.

I was so pathetic.

But Brant didn't seem to think so. "I love how responsive you are. Just wait until I get you alone." He nipped at my ear, and normally, I'd find that obnoxious, but somehow from Brant, I liked it.

"I don't want to wait. There's got to be a bathroom on this tub." I turned my face into his neck and nipped him back.

His grip around my waist tightened. "There is, but I don't have any latex."

"Why not?" My voice was a little higher pitched than I meant it to be.

"Because I didn't want to screw this up by trying to get in your pants."

"You blew past that one orgasm ago."

He laughed. "I guess I did. You were just too damn enticing and you smell like candy. What's a man to do?"

"If I smell like candy, I guess that means you should lick me." I teased.

"I guess I should." He put his hand to his lips and sucked his finger into his mouth. "Yeah, just like candy."

That might have been the most decadent thing I'd ever seen. I had to cross my legs as another tremor shot through me. I guess in the scheme of things, it wasn't that big a deal, but no one had ever done that after touching me. No one had ever been that enamored of me.

This feeling Brant wrought in me was addictive. I wanted more of it. Not just the pleasure, but the other things. Feeling wanted. Feeling beautiful.

"You're good with your mouth. Looks like you've had some practice." I nodded at him.

He laughed. "Is that your fantasy when you come to the club? Do you think we're all in the back oiling each other up and doing naughty things?"

"I know better. But it's kind of a hot picture, if I think about it."

"All the guys are convinced that when you have girls' night, they all go back to your place and you have a dirty slumber party."

"Oh really? Wouldn't you just like to know?"

"I would. You should tell me all about it."

Both his arms were around me and I inhaled the scent of him. From here on out, I'd associate Blue with orgasms. "I will. When you take me home."

"I didn't plan for this to happen. I really do want to get to know you, Claire."

"Are you saying you don't want to go home with me?"

"I'm saying I don't want to leave in the morning and never see you again."

"I never invite anyone to spend the night. I invited you." It was the closest I could come to any kind of promise.

"I'll make that concession. If you let me follow through on our breakfast plans."

It was a small thing, but I really liked that he used the word "concession." A good vocabulary always turned me on.

"Only because you used the word concession."

"I know."

Maybe he did get me after all.

FAT

CHAPTER THREE

When we got back to the house, I could hear April barking like a caffeinated purse dog all the way outside.

"Well, this isn't awkward at all." I said, standing in my living room.

Brant shrugged. "She's just having a good time."

"I'm not sure that I ever needed to know that about her though."

He grinned. "We could give them a run for their money."

"Oh yeah?"

"Yeah, baby." He moaned.

The howling stopped and the house was suddenly much too quiet. I dragged him into my room and shut the door, giggling. "What are you doing?"

"That thing you like." He made sure to project his voice so there could be no mistaking what he'd said through the walls.

FAT

It took me all of a nanosecond to decide to play along, Kieran had it coming. I couldn't count how many nights, mornings, or even afternoons I'd spent wearing my earphones trying to block out screams, moans, and a general carnal ruckus. Turnabout was finally fair play.

I moaned experimentally and the yipper dog was silent. I did it again and Brant banged into the wall with a snicker.

"Yeah, just like that," he growled.

"I didn't know I could bend that far. Harder."

He started banging a steady rhythm on the wall and I provided the soundtrack to accompany the show.

Only the next sound I made, he focused on me with a particular intensity. "You're really good at faking it. Makes me wonder what you sound like when you mean it," Brant whispered.

"You heard me on the boat."

"No, you were holding back because there were people around."

"There are people around now." My mouth was dry and I licked my lips. My feet carried me closer to him of their own accord.

"No one that actually cares what we're doing. This will be another story at the club just like the time Kieran banged that reporter in the dressing room. Instead, it'll be your turn to talk about how you and I rocked Kieran and his flavor of the day out of bed."

I didn't like how that sounded. I didn't want April to be the flavor of the day, even if that's what she signed up for. I didn't want the guys at the club to know I'd slept with Brant. But I did want Kieran to know for some screwed up reason. Maybe to highlight the fact I wasn't just his roommate, I wasn't actually one of the guys. I was a woman with needs.

And there was a man who wanted me, a man who thought I was hot, not in spite of being fat.

I didn't know how kissing was going to work, I could never picture it with a guy who was so much shorter than me. I always thought that I'd have to be the aggressor. But it was like dumping a bottle of mercury on a pane of glass--the molecules were drawn back toward each other. Our mouths were the same, the press of lips inevitable.

His hands were in my hair, on the nape of my neck, sliding down my arms, around my waist--it was as if he touched me everywhere at once.

Maybe he wasn't Mr. Right, but he could be Mr. Right Now.

I drew him to the bed and pulled his shirt over his head. It was nothing I hadn't seen before, but this was more intimate, this was real. What he did on stage was an act, there was no connection to anyone but himself.

He was working the zipper on the back of my dress and I froze. I didn't want him to see me naked.

"What's wrong?" His voice was low and ragged.

I didn't want to tell him because that would be even worse than being naked in front of him because I would be bare. Not just my skin, but me. Everything I wanted to keep hidden, even from myself.

"Change your mind? We can wait."

I was being stupid. It's not like my clothes hid that I was fat. It wasn't like he'd suddenly get me naked and it would be a surprise. He knew what he was getting into. Except part of me didn't believe that. Part of me still believed he'd be disgusted by me. Even though he'd chased me, even though he'd had his fingers between my thighs on the boat, and even though he was hard and had been all night.

"No, I didn't change my mind." I tilted my face up to kiss him again.

This time, he was tender, his kiss gentle. "I mean it, Claire. We can take our time."

I was such a fucking spaz. I wished I could be that confident, sexy woman I pretended to be. That everyone believed I was. I hated that I wasn't. To punish myself, I decided to confess. "I had a moment of self-doubt, but I'm over it."

He propped himself up on his elbows and searched my face. "About this? It's fine."

"No, about me. About..." I looked away from him. Yeah, this was why confession was a punishment. "About you wanting me after we took our clothes off."

Brant dipped his head and kissed my neck, sending shivers through me. "For being such a smart woman, that's a stupid thing for you to think. Can't you feel how much I want you?"

The self-doubt monkeys that were clawing their way up my back said that because he was a man, he'd fuck anything. He'd stick his dick anywhere because it was available, not because he wanted me. But that was stupid.

And cruel, both to me and to him. It painted him with an asshole brush that he'd never done anything to deserve.

"You're beautiful, Claire. You're sexy. You're smart. You're kind. You're everything."

His words felt good, but his hands felt even better. They were reverent and worshipful as they moved down my curves—a physical proof that what he said was true. I allowed him to peel my dress off and even in the dark, it was hard for me to look at him.

But he never stopped praising me as he undressed me. When I was naked, the look on his face was like he'd unwrapped some sort of treasure. It was like a drug and I was already addicted. I wanted to feel this way all the time. I never wanted that to stop.

I realized I was being selfish. I'd made this all about me and he seemed content to let me do that. I didn't deserve him. Not because of my body, but because I was here with him when I really wanted to be with Kieran.

It would serve me right if he'd really rather be there with April.

This was why I didn't date, this was why I didn't hook up. I could never just let go and enjoy the experience. I always had to pick everything to death and then pick at it some more.

I reached between us to unbutton his jeans.

"Condoms? We didn't stop and buy any."

"Nightstand."

He reached over me and grabbed one of the foil packets from the drawer. But he didn't rush, he kept kissing me as if we had all night, and I supposed we did. We had all the time in the world.

He had nowhere to go except here with me.

I ran my hands over his back, enjoying the texture of his skin. Smooth and warm, the hard planes of muscle rippling under my touch. I arched up against him, wanting to feel more of him. I couldn't get close enough. With the scent of Blue in my nose, I remembered the way he'd touched me on the boat. How I surrendered to that pleasure, to him.

He filled his hands with my breasts, his caress still unhurried and languid. It turned me on that he'd been so aroused, but still had iron control—that he wasn't rushing.

Another sound from Kieran's room shattered the web of desire he'd woven around me and I giggled again.

Brant didn't laugh this time. His eyes narrowed. "I take this as a personal challenge. In about five minutes, you're not going to care if the world ends, let alone what's going on in the next room."

I wondered what else he could possibly do to me because he'd already brought me off once.

His intentions became clear when he slid down between my thighs.

"I...that's not going to work."

"What do you mean, it's not going to work?"

I blushed, which was stupid. We couldn't get much more intimate, but it embarrassed me to talk about my orgasms, or lack thereof. "I'm not one of those multi-orgasmic women. I got one, so I'm going to be done until tomorrow."

"Whoever you've been with either didn't know what he was doing, or he was a selfish bastard completely unworthy of getting anywhere near this delicious body."

I swallowed hard. "Don't say I didn't warn you."

"Back at you." He gave me a nod that made me tremble. He was so confident, so sure of his own skill set that I couldn't help but believe him.

The first touch of his tongue was bliss, but I didn't think it would lead anywhere. It would be a bunch of build up for no payoff.

"Stop analyzing it. And making me talk with my mouth full."

I laughed, but decided to try just that. The strokes of his tongue against my clit were just as languid and unhurried as his kisses had been. That was sexy, that he wasn't just shooting for the end goal, that he enjoyed the journey rather than just the destination.

That helped me relax and enjoy what he was doing, rather than focusing only on the orgasm—just getting it done. I knew sex wasn't supposed to be like that, but I'd never forgotten my first boyfriend who ever went down on me telling me that it took too long. Or other guys who'd only paid it lip service—pun intended.

"What did I say? You're thinking too much. Feel it, Claire. I want you to get off, but enjoy the ride. Now, if I catch you thinking instead of feeling, I might have to spank you."

"Spank me? I'm no Anastasia."

But if he really wanted to spank me, I might try it. So far, this had all been about me. That was new and it made me wonder what else I'd been missing. I'd never felt so wanted—so desirable.

He didn't answer me, only moved his tongue faster and my brain finally shut down. At least the part that kept thinking about all the reasons why he didn't really want to be doing what he was doing.

Tendrils of pleasure wrapped themselves around me like vines, cradled me and threaded deep into my veins. It was as if our contact was deeper than skin, something secret and vital.

This time the build was slower, but more intense. I lost all sense of time and self, the only thing that mattered was sensation.

I thought I heard some guttural cries of bliss, but it wasn't April. It was me.

Only then did he rise above me, only then did he push himself inside. I clung to him, my nails digging into his back, my thighs locked around his hips, and the taste of my own pleasure in our kiss.

When he'd finished, he didn't roll off me and fall asleep like most of my other partners had. Brant was still inside me when he pushed my hair out of my face, stroked his fingers down my cheek and looked into my eyes for a long moment before kissing me softly. It wasn't passionless, but it wasn't lusty either. It was a different kind of kiss—one that spoke of intimacy and a connection.

It terrified me.

He gathered me against him and long after his breathing was deep and even, I lay awake staring into the darkness wondering what the hell I'd just done.

Besides having two orgasms for the first time.

CHAPTER FOUR

Brant wasn't in the bed next to me when I awoke, but his pillow was still warm and his shirt was still on the floor. He hadn't gone far and I wasn't sure how I felt about that. I wasn't sure how I felt about any of this.

I heard voices coming from the kitchen.

Wasn't that just going to be a bucket of awkward? We were all friends, or had been before last night. Kieran, April, Brant and I.

I really hoped April wasn't going to be one of the ones that I had to tell to go home. I'd been kidding last night, but Kieran didn't usually have morning coffee with the girls he brought home.

Unless April was something different for him.

That thought caused a pang of discomfort in my chest—and made me feel like the world's biggest asshole. My thighs were still sticky from sex with one guy and I was angsting over another. Why did I do this shit to myself?

I thought about hiding in my room until everyone went home, but Kieran was already home. I'd have to face him sooner or later. But later was good...

No, it actually wasn't. I needed to own my shit. Facing them later wouldn't change what anyone had to say about anything. Further, I was a grown-up capable of making my own choices, up to and including who I decided to sleep with. Kieran had been pushing me toward Brant for a while. What did he expect would happen?

I got up and pulled on a pair of jeans and a Day of the Dead t-shirt, stuffed my hair up into a reasonable facsimile of a ponytail and padded out to the kitchen for a cup of coffee.

Brant smiled and handed me a cup. One packet of Stevia and cream, just the way I liked it.

"Thanks." I accepted the cup gratefully. I watched him over the rim of the cup, and his smile was infectious. Not only because he really was handsome, but it reminded me of all the wonderful things he could do with his mouth.

"You're much too fucking chipper this morning, boy-o." Kieran mumbled as he guzzled his black coffee.

Brant turned to Kieran to reply and that's when April and I both saw the angry, red scratches down his back. He looked like he'd been wrestling bears or something. I almost choked on my coffee when I realized *I'd* done that to him.

April squealed and flashed me a look. I wasn't sure if it was supposed to be props or censure.

Brant, on the other hand, didn't care which. He flashed a grin over his shoulder. "Oh, that. Yeah. Battle scars." He winked at me. "They're a good look, don't you think?"

I blushed. "You have to work tonight. I'm so sorry."

"No worries. I'll get better tips. Men don't look like they've tangled with a hellcat if they're bad at what they do." He winked again.

"Well, you know, if it helps, you should come over after work and I'll give you some more." This time I thought it was Kieran who was going to choke on his coffee. That gave me some perverse sense of satisfaction. "I mean, in the name of your career. I like helping my friends."

"You could help the shit out of me," Kieran said.

FAT

His words slammed into me. What was I supposed to do with that? Was this part of our usual banter, or did he mean it? I shook my head, maybe because I thought if I rattled my brain around enough, something might start making sense. Before I decided I wanted Kieran, I never would have questioned that. So why start now? Suddenly wanting him wasn't some kind of alchemy that could change what always was or *wasn't* between us.

"I guess you could take a number and get in line." I decided to play it off.

April looked hurt, but Brant just smirked. "You haven't got the skills to elicit that kind of reaction. *Boy-o*." He tossed Kieran's Irish affectation back at him. "Give it as many tries as she'll let you."

I liked his confidence. I could tell from the way he held himself, the look on his face, everything about him said that he wasn't talking shit—that he believed what he said.

"Riddle me this," April interjected. "What's it like when you two have sex? I'm trying to picture it and the only thing that comes to mind is a Chihuahua trying to mount a Great Dane."

Her words were a barbed arrow that struck home for me, but Brant was singularly unfazed.

He snorted. "A Chihuahua? Have you ever heard yourself?" Brant then mimicked the sounds we'd heard last night coming from Kieran's room. He yipped, barked, and sounded an ineffectual little howl that did indeed sound like a Chihuahua that had been taking hits from a helium tank.

"Fuck you, Brant." April poured herself a refill.

"Not if you paid me." The retort was quick, sharp and from the look on her face, had obviously struck home much as her words had done to me. "So, you guys want to get breakfast?" He changed the subject.

"I could go for a steak. How about you, Taco Bell?" Kieran looked at April. "You want some breakfast?"

For a second, I wondered if I heard him correctly. If he'd just called her Taco Bell in reference to the little Chihuahua mascot the chain had once had.

Instead of being pissed, she blushed. "Yeah, I guess."

"Get your ass in gear." He swatted her ass and she scurried off to put on something besides his t-shirt.

I hated her in that moment. Not just because she was wearing his shirt, but that was a contributing factor. No, actually, it wasn't. I was jealous, to be sure, but I couldn't be angry at two people who fucked because they wanted to. Neither of them owed me fidelity.

But what April did owe me was friendship. Not even something so trite as Girl Code, but Friend Code. She knew how self-conscious I was about being with someone smaller than me. She knew it, and she used it against me because the guy she wanted was giving his attention to me instead of her.

Even though she was the one he'd fucked last night. She was the one in his bed. She was the one wearing his t-shirt. She was the one who had what I wanted.

Brant finished his coffee in one swallow. "I'm going to get dressed. Don't take too long with that coffee. I can buy you another."

"Yeah, but you made this one for me. So I want this one."

"If you tore up my back like that, I'd make you coffee every day." Kieran grinned.

"You had your chance, *Oirish*." Brant mocked him, but clapped a hand on his shoulder. "Snooze you lose." He wandered back toward my room leaving us alone.

"I guess last night went really well," Kieran said.

What to say? I usually told him everything, but I couldn't tell him this. Not what I really felt about any of it. "Yeah, I guess it did. You were right. Brant is a nice guy."

"You deserve a nice guy." He nodded. "Gavin went home with Rosa."

"No shit?" I couldn't picture that. Not after the things he'd said about me being pretty for a fat girl. Rosa was the same size as me. Gorgeous, but not skinny. Not traditionally beautiful, as I'd come to say.

"Yeah. I bet that's going to be an awkward morning."

"Probably no more awkward than this one. It's a little weird, you have to admit."

"Nah." Kieran shook his head. "It'd be weird if we'd had a foursome. That's when it gets awkward."

I was determined not to blush. Although, I wasn't sure if I succeeded or not. "I don't see that happening."

"Try harder. It could be fun." He grinned.

"It's always about sex with you."

"It's always about sex with everyone, Claire. Don't let anyone try to fool you and say that it isn't."

I couldn't let that go, even though logic said to ignore it and move along. "What about us? We're friends. I like to think that we care about each other. Am I wrong?"

"Of course I care about you."

Okay, now would have been a good time to let it go. But my mouth kept moving. "We've never had sex. What does fucking have to do with us?"

He grabbed me hard, hugged me. For one moment, I allowed myself to think about the way his body felt under my hands, my breasts crushed into the hard expanse of his chest—his hands burning my skin through my t-shirt.

God, it was like I'd gone from Lolly Librarian to some kind of sex addict.

"It's *because* I care about you, because I love you. But don't think for one minute that I don't know you're a woman." He released me as suddenly as he'd grabbed me and then rinsed out his cup as if that hadn't just happened.

My brain overloaded with scenarios. Of all the times we could have fallen into bed if one of us had made a move. He wanted me, too.

I didn't believe it. It didn't make sense. Kieran Holt could have any woman on the planet. Why would he choose me?

He wouldn't. It was just because for the whole of the time we'd been roommates, he'd never seen me with another guy. The few guys I had dated briefly didn't come to the house, we didn't hang out together as a group and Brant was in our group of friends. I'd always still been his friend... These guys I dated were never real to him.

I knew Kieran had attachment/abandonment issues. He'd been on his own since he was fourteen. No one had ever stuck with him like I had. I was his family.

"Are you going to wear that to breakfast?" he asked.

"Uh—" I looked down at myself. "Yeah. Is there something wrong with it?"

"No. If you're ready you can tell April to get moving."

I really didn't want her to come. I wanted her to go home so she'd know she was nothing better than any of the other warm, wet holes Kieran had in his bedroom. She wasn't special. For once, I didn't want her to get what she wanted. Because I'm an asshole. I hated feeling that way about my friend, but I couldn't seem to stop. "You know, if all you wanted to give her was Finn McCool, you shouldn't be taking her out to breakfast."

"She's taking me."

I rolled my eyes. "You know what I mean."

"She says she wants the Kieran experience. The real me. I kind of don't believe her. She just wants me because she thinks she can't have me."

"Can she have you?" I really wanted him to say no. I wanted him to say that he could never belong to anyone but me.

"Anyone who wants me can have me, lass. I'm nothing special."

"Finn McCool thinks he's pretty damn special." I teased.

"Finn McCool knows he's not good for anything but his dick. We all have our talents, love, and that's his."

I bit my lip. I'd never heard him talk this way before. "Kieran Holt is worth a lot more than Finn McCool. He's pretty, there's no doubt about that. But you're my best friend. Do you really think that if all you had to offer was a handsome face and a nice gun show that I'd trust you to live in my house? That it would be your shoulder I lean on?"

"And here I thought you just liked hugging me because I'm taller than you." That moment of insecurity, wherever it had come from, was gone. In its place was the Kieran I knew so well.

Then I wondered if maybe he was just as damaged as me. I'd always admired him for how he'd come through so much, but lived life on his own terms. He wouldn't be content with what the world gave him, he reached out and took what he wanted. Only maybe, he hid his insecurities the same way I hid mine. He was just better at it.

"April is taking a damn long time. I'll go hurry her along. I'm starved." I wasn't really, I hated eating in the morning. Kieran knew that. But I had to get away from the situation and the things it made me feel.

I wandered into Kieran's room and found April sitting on the bed. "What are you doing?"

She looked up at me. "Feeling horrible."

"For what?" If she said she regretted telling Kieran she wanted the real him instead of Finn McCool, I might slap her.

"For what I said."

My hand twitched.

"About the Chihuahua and Great Dane. That was super shitty."

I exhaled heavily. So she knew what she'd said was mean. I didn't know which was worse. If she'd known it and done it anyway, or was completely oblivious. "It's okay. All the women Kieran brings home are threatened by me because I'm permanent and they want to be." Yeah, maybe I was being a little shitty myself.

"I know," she admitted. "It pissed me off when he started talking about wanting you to scratch him. I mean, we'd just had sex *again*. I gave him the BJ of my life, but obviously not his, the way he was talking about you."

Ouch. If I were April, I'd be hurt too. "You know that he and I are friends. Best friends. We've always had that kind of banter and we always will. If he's really the one for you, that shouldn't matter."

"I don't know if I have the stones to be with a guy like him. He's so hot and he could have any woman he wants. Why would he pick me?"

A gamut of emotions washed over me. I'd just been saying the same things in my own head. *Why, indeed?* "Well, you should have thought about that before you told him you wanted him for himself. He's not perfect, April. He has doubts, and insecurities. We all do, even guys that look like him. And I guess even women who look like you, too. Have you seen yourself lately?"

"I guess there is always someone who is going to be prettier, smarter and skinnier."

Back to that again. "Why do you assume that skinnier is always better? Why can't someone just want to be with you because you're you?"

"Because it doesn't work that way." April sighed.

"Really? You just said that to me?" I thought about what Kieran had said. That he was definitely aware I was a woman. That he hadn't tried to get in my pants because he loved me.

April worried her lip and I could see that she was conflicted, but after what she'd just said, I didn't really care. "Hurry up. Don't be that chick who doesn't go home."

She looked like I'd just hit her and I might as well have. "He invited me to breakfast."

"Of course he did. We're all going. So you can't very well sit here in his room while we go eat, can you?"

She pushed her feet into her shoes. "Yeah, I'm coming."

I could have been nicer, but if no one else cared about my feelings, why should I worry about dancing around hers?

I knew this would happen. As soon as he started shagging my friends, things would go straight to shit.

I almost wished it had been anyone but April. She was the "pretty girl" who got everything. Everyone wanted to be her, know her, or fuck her. I was jealous, I could admit that. Who wouldn't be? If the universe had been listening to me, Gavin and April would have gone home together.

But I wasn't the girl whose wishes came true. I was more like the Wicked Witch. I had to plot, scheme, and claw for every bit of good that came my way.

Which was a reminder I should have been working on *Chubbalicious* rather than worrying about any of this crap.

Now I had to go sit through a breakfast which I'm sure was going to be awkward and uncomfortable. I'd rather just go back to my room and work on the website.

Except when I came out of Kieran's room, Brant was waiting for me and all my anxiety vanished. I don't know why he had that effect on me, but he did. Everything seemed simpler when he was around. It was as if his very presence was like a dose of *bitch, be cool.*

"Where do you want to go?"

"I thought we were going to IHOP?"

He shrugged. "If that's where you want to go."

"You're being too nice to me." Mostly because I felt like I didn't deserve it.

He raised a brow. "Do you think I should treat you badly? Claire, I haven't done anything for you I wouldn't do for any of my friends."

"If you treat your friends this way, I can't imagine how you treat your girlfriends."

Brant eyed me like he wanted to say something, but he didn't. I probably shouldn't have brought up the subject of girlfriends anyway, considering I'd told him I didn't want any kind of commitment.

April emerged from the bedroom and I saw she still wore Kieran's shirt and a pair of his boxers-like shorts. She'd managed to snag a pair of my sneakers and her hair was tucked up in a bouncy ponytail. "Ready."

"I'll drive," Kieran offered.

"Did we decide where we were going?" Brant asked.

"The usual. Unless the girls want something else."

"I'm just going to have more coffee, so whatever Claire wants," April demurred.

I wasn't going to let her keep me from eating, even if all she had was coffee. I wasn't going to be one of those girls who didn't eat because she was with a man. I nodded and we shuffled into the backseat of Kieran's Challenger.

It was a tight fit, but Brant had no qualms about pulling me into his lap. Probably because my breasts were shoved into his chin.

"Jesus, Claire. Are you trying to kill him?" April joked.

It hadn't occurred to me until now how often April said things like that. How often she poked at my weight, or my size, or anything else that she knew I was sensitive about. I acted like I didn't care, so maybe she thought I really didn't.

"Hey, if I die, I'll die happy." His hand splayed on my hip pulled me closer.

"I'd rather you didn't die."

"Would you miss me?" He nuzzled into my neck.

It was a different experience to be the one who had the gushy morning after PDA. To be the one who was the center of someone's attention.

"Maybe." I cupped his jaw and leaned down close to his ear. "I'd definitely miss your tongue," I whispered so only he could hear me.

Kieran tapped the brakes abruptly. "Hey, none of that back there." I met his eyes in the rearview mirror. "I don't want any white stains on my black interior."

"It's leather. It'll come up with a wet wipe," Brant replied.

"Ewww." April shivered in her seat. "We don't need to be that close."

"That's not close. If you were back there too, *that* would be close," Kieran added.

"You joke about that all the time. I think you're really angling for a foursome," I teased.

"Why not? We're all friends." Kieran was stone-faced.

"Because Brant already said he wouldn't fuck me if I paid him and that would leave just you and Claire. I'm sure if you wanted to, you would have already done it by now. So, that takes that off the table." April said this without rancor and for a moment, it was like we were back in familiar territory—territory where we weren't sniping at each other over dick.

For some reason, that brought to mind what Kieran had said—that he was only good for his body, his cock. My gaze was drawn back to him, but he wasn't watching the road. He was watching me in the mirror again.

"Sure, why not?" I rolled my eyes.

"Really?" Brant whispered in my ear. "Who do you want to fuck? April or Kieran?"

My face flamed. "I was being sarcastic."

"Were you?" He wasn't judging me. No, not by a long shot. He was turned on. The ridge of his erection pressed into my leg.

"You're a little twisted."

"A little?" He leaned closer. "If you knew the things I've already watched you do in my head…"

"You're so wrong." But I giggled like I was twelve.

"Sometimes, you have to be wrong to be right."

"So this orgy… tonight work for everyone?" Kieran's tone was casual.

"I have to work tomorrow, so no good for me." April was just as cavalier.

"On a Sunday?" I asked.

"Yeah. My boss is being a douche. He wants a new proposal by Monday, and I mean, I guess I could have worked on it Friday, but it was my birthday. I'm only going to be twenty-four once."

"No, when you're thirty, you'll try twenty-four again." Kieran grinned.

"Of course I will, but it won't be the same. The people we are right now, at this minute, we'll never be again. Half an hour from now, we won't be the same because we've had other experiences, stimuli. Every moment we're given is unique and can never be repeated."

"That's pretty fucking profound," I agreed.

She was right. I wasn't the same person I'd been last night, none of us were. Every experience changes our perceptions. Maybe it wasn't noticeable, but it was like a river cutting through rock. Because of the constant wear, that rock was never exactly the same shape it'd been even minutes before. The changes were miniscule, but they were changes nonetheless.

"Every once in a while, I'm good for something."

That sounded a lot like what Kieran had said. Maybe they were right for each other.

"I was reading something last night that said you should never say anything about yourself that you don't want to be true," Brant said.

"You read?" April snorted.

"Of course I read. Your buddy Gavin isn't the only one doing this gig to pay for school. You think I want to do this forever? That any of us do?"

"I'll do it until I break a hip, maybe even after. I love this job," Kieran offered.

"I didn't say I don't love it, but it's like anything that relies on your physicality. Eventually, you get old. In this business, middle-aged might as well be dead."

"What are you going for?" I asked him.

"Biomedical science. I'm interested in research."

And here all I wanted to do was design clothes.

"Biomedical science? Really?" April turned all the way around in her seat. "And here I thought you were just a pretty face. Have you thought about your investment portfolio?"

"Actually, I have. I invest half of what I make at the club."

And I had all of my money tied up in *Chubbalicious*. If it failed, I was fucked, not to put too fine a point on it. "I don't think you're supposed to be that together at twenty-three, Brant."

"He's obviously not because he's not with Bausch." April teased.

"Landell gave me an extra percent." He shrugged, referring to their biggest competitor.

"I could have fixed that for you. Why don't you come in and see me this week about your portfolio? We'll see if I can get you better terms."

No, no and more no. April had Kieran, she didn't get to have Brant too. She saw he was making money, he was smart, he could play in her league and now suddenly she was interested in his "portfolio"? Yeah, right.

"I'm pretty happy where I am." He pressed his lips against my neck.

I shouldn't have felt like that was such a victory, but I did.

CHAPTER FIVE

After breakfast, Kieran dropped April at her car and Brant seemed to take that as his cue to leave as well.

I was surprised that I didn't want him to go, but he had a paper he had to finish. We agreed to see each other next Saturday and go out after the photoshoot for *Chubbalicious*. Both Rosa and Hollie texted to say they were game. Everything was coming together.

"See, didn't I tell you that you guys would hit it off?" Kieran said and poured himself a cup of cold coffee left over from the morning.

"We did. He is a nice guy." I bit my lip.

"But?"

"But nothing." I shrugged.

"When you bite your lip like that, there's always a but."

"I'm terrified, okay?"

"Of what? Did he do something shitty, because if he did..." He let the threat hang in the air.

"No, nothing like that. I like him." But I knew I was going to fuck it up because of my feelings for Kieran. I couldn't even tell him about that part.

"Is there someone else?"

I should've known I wouldn't be able to hide much from him. We'd been friends too long. "I don't know." I bit my lip harder, trying to keep those words inside my mouth. "Maybe."

"You should tell him."

"Which him?" If I bit my lip any more, I was going to bite through it.

"The guy you think you have feelings for."

"Why would I do that? If he wanted me, he's had plenty of opportunity to tell me."

"The same could be said about you," he said pointedly.

"It doesn't work that way. I'm the female. The male pursues."

"Why does it work that way? Why is all the pressure on us?" Kieran sat on the couch and I plopped down beside him. "Is it someone I know? Does he work at the club? You know it's different for dancers. You have to tell us if you want something from us."

"Brant didn't need me to tell him anything." I liked that about him. I liked a lot of things about him. It made me wish that sitting this close to Kieran didn't make my hands clammy and my heart race like the flutter of hummingbird wings.

"That's Brant. He's a different breed all together. None of the other guys at the club are good enough for you anyway."

I didn't know what to say to that, so I changed the subject. When in doubt, talk about something—anything—else. "Thanks for agreeing to do the shoot with the girls for *Chubbalicious*."

"Anything for you, Claire-bear."

Anything for me? If only. I bit my lip again and winced because it actually hurt. "Damn it."

He laughed.

"I'm glad my pain amuses you." I snatched the remote and turned on the DVR. We had episodes of American Horror Story to gorge on.

"Stop chewing your lips, lass. Then it won't hurt." He put his arm around me like he'd done every Saturday afternoon since we became roommates.

But something was different.

I was different.

And he could tell. "What's this now?" His accent grew thicker, but I couldn't tell if it was because he was relaxed, or he was trying. "Shagging Brant doesn't mean you're not still my bird."

I laughed. "I am definitely not your bird after last night. It was April who was singing."

"She wasn't the only one."

"I'm not apologizing. I figure all those nights I had to sleep with earphones, you had it coming."

"I had *her* coming."

I rolled my eyes. "I should have expected that one."

For the briefest second, everything was normal again. He wasn't the embodiment of any fantasy, he was just my friend. He was Kieran.

"Yeah, you should've. Now come here." Even though I was already next to him, he pulled me even closer. "You're too far away."

I knew exactly what he meant. A distance between us now that wasn't physical, but it was there nonetheless and I didn't know if it was something that could be fixed. A switch had been flipped and like April said, we'd never be the same.

After a long pause he spoke, "If you don't want me to see April again, I won't."

The thrill that shot through me was so wrong. So very wrong. A part of me was tempted to say that I never wanted him to breathe the same air as she did. But that was ridiculous, immature, and petty. All things I didn't want to be.

"Why would you say that?" I ventured.

"Seeing April is the only thing I can think of that would change us, and we *are* changed. I don't like it." He sighed. "That was the one thing you asked of me—that I not shag your friends."

"Kieran—" my sigh matched his "—I want you to be happy. If April makes you happy, then be with her." Those words might as well have been razorblades on my tongue. I did want him to be happy. I just didn't want it to be her that made him happy.

Who was I kidding? I wanted it to be me, and now he'd handed me all this power. I still wasn't happy because he didn't want me the way he wanted April. He needed me, he loved me, but he didn't *want* me.

Meatloaf was wrong. Two out of three was all kinds of bad.

"She's not what I want."

Relief splashed like cold water on a sunburn. "What *do* you want?"

"It's so far away, I don't even dare name it."

Something nagging at the back of my brain told me not to push this one, but I wanted to encourage him. "There's nothing stopping you."

"Only my good sense."

"I've never let that stop me. I mean, how insane is *Chubbalicious*?"

He turned to look at me. "It's not insane at all. It's fucking brilliant. There are a lot of curvier women who want to dress up, who want to feel good doing it. You're going to give that to them. Supply and demand."

"But is it going to be enough to support myself? I dropped out of college. I'm going both feet first. What if I fail?"

"Then you'll go back to university. You'll get loans. But you won't fail. The shoot Saturday is marketing genius."

"Thanks for believing in me." How had this turned into a conversation about me? "You know that I'm here for you, too, right?" I put my hand on his.

"I know and I hope I never lose that."

"Why would you think you could?" My heart thudded and trepidation snaked around my ribs squeezing ever tighter.

"Because I fuck up everything I touch. I get it dirty and then I break it."

"That's bullshit. Don't say that." There was so much pain in his words made all the more poignant because he really believed it to be true. The sky was blue. The grass was green. Kieran broke things. It was an absolute in his mind.

I tilted my head to look up at him and turned his face toward me. I wanted him to see the truth in my eyes when I spoke.

"You don't dirty anything. You don't break things. Other people break themselves on you and that's their cross to bear. Not yours. Never apologize for surviving. Or for being who you are."

The intimacy of our position hit me hard. Intimacy between us was commonplace, but not like this. I'd cupped his jaw when I turned him to face me and his hand was in my hair. If this were any other couple, a crashing of mouths was what would happen next.

But it wasn't any other couple.

It was me. It was Kieran.

My lips parted and I was vaguely aware that I'd wet them in expectation. I'd have blushed at the trajectory of my thoughts, if I'd remembered to breathe. It was like we were underwater, everything moving in slow-motion.

For a nanosecond, I thought he was going to kiss me.

He dipped his head slowly, his green eyes gone dark like the cold Irish sea, his lips parted.

And oh Jesus, I was dying. Expectation, desire, fear—everything it was possible to feel rolled over me in wave after wave. My belly tightened and I was afraid if he did kiss me, I might shatter right there in his arms.

But if he didn't…that would break me too.

He buried his face in my neck, his hand still tangled in my hair, and his breath hot and taunting on my skin.

Shame burned. Of course he wasn't going to kiss me. I knew he didn't want me that way. It was April and girls like her. After all, Kieran could have anyone he wanted. Why would he ever choose me?

I closed my eyes and wrapped my arms around him. "It's okay, Kieran." I had no idea what I was telling him was okay. Maybe I was really telling myself that it was okay for me to have had that stupid thought, that demon hope.

Even now, my body ached for him, knowing there was no chance for anything more. My stupid brain stored up every touch. The way it felt to be with him like this, that magnetism between us I'd imagined—all for my pretty little fantasy world.

Why did I do this to myself?

I stroked his hair, enjoying the silky texture. I tried to concentrate on that, on something that would calm my breathing. He had to feel the slam of my heart against my ribs, it was almost like it was trying to jackhammer from my flesh into his.

His heart beat wildly, too. His breath was a staccato rhythm against my throat.

Maybe he'd been afraid I'd try to kiss him and he didn't know how to tell me no. Even that thought wasn't enough to make me let go of him, to surrender this moment to the past. It was mine. I was going to hold on to it as long as he'd let me.

"If only you knew."

"I do know. I do," I assured him.

He broke the embrace. "The shoot Saturday. You told Brant that you'd do some scenes with him. Do one with me."

"What?" That was the last thing I'd expected him to say.

"You're the designer. You should have shots with all of us."

"I'm not putting them on the site."

"You might change your mind. Then you'll have them."

That little voice in the back of my head screamed no, that this was the bad idea to end all bad ideas. But what could it hurt? It wasn't like I was going to actually put them up.

"Okay."

Except after I said it, I felt like I'd just triggered some series of events that would cause the apocalypse.

But that was dumb. It was just a couple of pictures on a car.

We settled in and rewound the episode to catch what we'd missed. Except I couldn't pay attention to what was happening on the screen—as much as I wanted to. I was hyperaware of everywhere we touched. Of the way he smelled—like Polo Black. The heat of him.

I felt like the biggest asshole.

Not only because I'd spent the night previous with Brant—I'd told him I didn't want any sort of relationship or commitment. Even though I still felt guilty sitting here perving on Kieran. But because he'd turned to me as a friend, he needed me and I was too busy worrying about my pussy and the size of my ass.

Really, Claire? I asked myself—as if somehow asking the question might change the answer.

When the episode was over, he kissed the top of my head. So not what I'd been angling for. "I'm going to crash for a few hours. It's going to be a late night."

"See you later."

"You could come." He waggled his brows.

"Watch you sleep? No thanks."

"No, you could do that little hair twirl you were doing earlier. It would put me right to sleep. Maybe pet my eyebrows?"

"That's a girlfriend job. If I have to do the work, I want the perks." Fuck, why had I said that? My mouth was going to get me in more trouble yet.

He looked like I'd just punched him. "What exactly are the perks you're referring to?"

"I have no idea. I was just talking shit." Honesty might actually work here.

"You think on that and let me know."

What was wrong with me? He'd invited me to go to bed with him. This was what I wanted. Why had I said no? He didn't want to fuck me, but shouldn't I take what I could get—I mean, if he was offering?

That petty part of me spoke up again. She said that this was the thing I had over every other woman who came into his life—including April. I had this side of him. It was mine.

"I'll pet you to sleep, but you owe me dinner. And change the sheets," I blurted before I could chicken out.

"Done. I changed them before we left."

Ha. April had been scrubbed away as easy as that. I knew it was wrong of me to think of it like that. Hell, everything I'd done in the last twenty four hours was wrong, but I did it anyway.

I followed him into his room and my hands were sweaty, my stupid pulse racing. I was just going to take a nap. We'd done this before too. This wasn't any new territory.

Kicking off my shoes, I got on the bed with all the trepidation of a virgin on prom night. He wrapped himself around me, his head on my chest just above my breasts.

And I stroked his hair as promised, smoothed my thumb over his eyebrows. It was an odd thing to find comforting, but he said his mother had done it when he was little.

When his breathing was deep and even, I didn't stop touching him. I kept curling locks of his hair over my fingers, stroking my hand down his biceps, his back, enjoying the free rein I had with his body.

Every now and again he made a low rumbling sound that I swear could've been a purr. I wondered if all guys in Ireland were like Kieran. If so, I could never go there. My panties would explode.

I thought about Brant—about how good he made me feel. About how I didn't have this trepidation with him. Spending time with him, being with him, it was easy. Kieran, even if he did feel the same way about me, not so much. He was a more complicated creature.

He shifted in his sleep, his hand falling dangerously close to my breast.

I wanted him to touch me, but I wanted him to do it because he wanted to, not because he was half asleep and I was a warm body. I turned on my side and his hand moved to my ass.

Of course it did.

I looked down at his face. His black lashes dusted his cheeks and a rebellious lock of hair curled down over his forehead. He was as beautiful as any work of art in the Nelson-Atkins. It was almost painful to look at him.

He still wasn't Finn McCool. He was Kieran.

Kieran who buried his face in my cleavage. I was almost worried he was going to smother himself, but I wouldn't deny it was nice having him there.

He'd said he knew I was a woman—meaning he wasn't unaware of my assets.

A stray seed of hope bloomed. Maybe I could have him after all, but what would that mean for our friendship? What if it didn't work out?

And what about Brant?

This felt too right to worry about that.

Until I saw April's panties on the floor. Her tiny, lacy, delicate, pink panties that she'd worn for her night with Finn Fucking McCool.

Bile churned and I hated everything. I hated the way I'd acted, the thoughts in my head, my emotions—I felt like a total fucking psycho.

I suddenly couldn't stand for Kieran to touch me. He'd been touching someone else, fucking someone else, but he came to me to feel safe? But I wasn't safe at all.

I untangled myself slowly, easing away from him. Part of me wanted him to wake up, to notice I was leaving, but he didn't. He scrounged in the bed and was still. As if I'd never been there.

I poured a glass of wine, grabbed my Kindle and ran a hot bath. Sinking into the heat, I let the bubbles and wine leach away my stress and I lost myself in a Virginia Nelson novel. After I'd finished it, I put my Kindle to the side and ran some more hot water.

She was my go-to read for happily ever after. I kind of wished she'd write my life story because then I'd know that after all of this bullshit, that I'd end up exactly where I was supposed to be with exactly who I was supposed to be with.

And I definitely had my doubts.

Why couldn't I be in love with Brant? That would make things so much easier.

I suppose I hadn't even given myself or him a chance. Not really. I was pining over Kieran, which was an absolute waste of time.

All of this was. I should get my head straight and work on *Chubbalicious*. The rest of this could wait. I still needed to finish the alterations for Hollie's dresses and I only had a week.

My phone rang. It was April. I didn't want to answer it. I'd just fixed my brain to where it was in a workable place, but I knew she'd keep calling until I answered. I considered turning it off, but then I'd wonder what she wanted, or when she was going to show up because I *hadn't* answered.

"What are you doing?"

"In the bath."

"Come over."

"I can't. I've got to finish these alterations."

"From the bath?" she asked.

I narrowed my eyes. "Obviously not. I was taking a break with some wine, some Virginia and some bubbles."

"Rosa is still at Gavin's. I think they really hit it off. We need to plot to find someone for Hollie."

"Well, I was going to pair her with Austin for the shoot. She likes the cowboys."

"That's brilliant." She was silent for a long moment. "So, I was a bitch earlier."

"Me too, maybe just a little." I didn't want to fight with her. I loved her. And that was as close to an apology as either of us would get.

But did I love her more than Kieran? No. I didn't.

"After Kieran leaves tonight, do you think you could grab my panties? I forgot them."

I'd seen dozens of girls use that as an excuse to come back over in hopes it would lead to something more. It was interesting that she asked me to get them for her. "Do we need to be that close?"

"Yes. I know that's a girl-that-won't-go-home technique. I really didn't do it on purpose. I just didn't want to put them back on after...well. Yeah."

"So now you're asking me to pick up your crispy panties?" I snorted.

"You can use a baggie. It won't kill you."

"It might, it just might." I remembered how the sight of them turned my stomach.

"Please? I wouldn't bother if they were cheap, but those are real silk. I got them in Paris on my senior trip."

"Fine." I hated the word as soon as it was out of my mouth.

"You're the best." She sighed. "Don't think I wasn't tempted to come over and get them myself."

"Then why don't you?"

"Because I told Kieran I was different, and I am."

"I've got to go. My bathwater is getting cold."

"You're still not coming over later?" she prodded.

"No."

"I guess I'll have to go to The Rooster by myself tonight."

"Why are you going back?" A sinking feeling in my gut told me I'd be going too.

"Because I want to prove to him that I can handle his job. That I won't freak out on any girl who tries to put her hand in his jock. You should come too, I mean, if you and Brant are dating."

"We're not."

"What are you doing? Just fucking?"

It sounded bad the way she said it—dripping with derision. I wouldn't call it "just fucking". There was more to it than that and I suddenly felt protective of what Brant and I had. It wasn't a relationship, per se, but it wasn't some sordid thing either. And I didn't want to share the details of that with her.

"I don't know, but I'm not going to show up at The Rooster and crawl up his ass." That would set a bad precedent anyway. He had a paper to write, we'd agreed to see each other next week, I didn't want to spend every minute with him. Neither did I want to deal with my feelings for Kieran tonight.

Going to the club would just make me feel bad about myself and reiterate all the doubts in my head on some demon loop from hell that I couldn't unhear. I had better things to do.

"I don't think he'd see it that way."

"Why isn't Hollie going with you?" I didn't know why I tried to argue. I knew I was going.

"She's got a thing with her sister. Come on, I don't want to go by myself."

"Why not? If this is all well and good, why not go by yourself?"

"Because I think I lied. I don't know if I can handle it."

Her confession did me in. I wanted to say no, I wanted to say that was her tough luck and to deal with it, but I couldn't. I just couldn't. "Fine." I hated that word. "Pick me up at ten."

"You're the best, Claire. I love you."

"Yeah, yeah. I've got to go. See you later." I hung up before she could respond.

Why in the name of all that was holy did I allow myself to get talked into these things?

CHAPTER SIX

I waited for Kieran to leave before I emerged from my room.

April's panties were on the counter.

That was completely unsanitary and made me wonder what other things he'd been putting on the counter.

As well as wondering if he'd heard my conversation with her. Not that it mattered.

Okay, that was a lie. He'd have to have been standing outside the bathroom door to hear me and that mattered quite a bit, but I couldn't think—i.e. obsess—about that now.

I decided to wear crop pants, flats and a cute bowling shirt. It had a '57 cherry red Chevy on it and it made my boobs look amazing. Of course, I always thought they looked amazing. It was hard to go wrong with boobs.

The bell rang promptly at ten.

A sick feeling settled in my gut. This was such a bad idea. *Bad. Bad. Bad.*

I opened the door and April was dressed to kill. She was wearing a tiny leather miniskirt that I could have used for a garter, a filmy see-through club halter, and those designer heels with the red sole.

"Wow."

"Do you think he'll like it?"

"Who wouldn't?"

"You look great, too. I love that shirt on you." April smiled.

I knew she was trying to be nice, but I didn't want her to be nice.

"Ready?" I didn't invite her in.

"Um, are those my panties on your counter?" She pursed her lips.

"Yeah. Kieran left them there."

"I see." Her expression was unreadable. "Let me just grab them and save you the baggie."

"Did you tell him you were coming tonight?"

"Of course. I told him *and Brant* you were coming too."

"We're not sitting by the stage. We're not going to be those girls."

She looked at me after she'd stuffed her panties in her purse. "What do you mean?"

"You know. The ones that want to put their stamp on the guys and keep other girls from getting their fantasy. But that's how they make their money."

"It's not even like that. I want him to see me, to know I'm there."

"He will. Especially since you told him you're coming. I think going tonight is a bad idea anyway." The word bad kept flashing with neon blinkers behind my eyes—a kind of warning I would regret ignoring.

"How else will I be able to prove to him I can handle his job?"

"Go next week. This is too soon. It's like calling the day you get his phone number. It's desperate."

"You're weird, you know that, right?" April eyed me. "Why do you care so much about what other people think?"

It occurred to me that women like April didn't have the same rules as the rest of us. She was so used to getting who and what she wanted, it would never enter her brain that there were rules to the hunt.

I shrugged. "Hey, I just live with the man."

"Did he say anything about me?"

Aside from the part where he'd stop seeing you if I wanted him to? "No. We did our usual Saturday thing. We watched American Horror Story and took a nap."

"Together?" Her eyes narrowed.

"Yeah, together. What about it?"

She bit her lip. "Why haven't you guys fucked? You have all the hallmarks of a relationship. You do everything together." I heard what sounded like defeat in her tone.

"Because we're just friends." The words tasted like poison, both because what had happened this afternoon had been something different and I was ready to throw away our honest friendship because I was suddenly obsessed with his dick.

And more than that, I realized. I was obsessed with the idea that a guy like him could want a girl like me.

Someone with a perfect body could be aroused by someone with an imperfect body. I wanted to prove it to myself, and everyone else.

"So says you until you fall into bed. You can't say you're not attracted to him. I mean, no sane, heterosexual woman could not want to ride Kieran Holt like a mechanical bull."

"I have never denied he's hot." She was interrogating me and I was about to defend our relationship to her like her opinion had any bearing on the matter. So I clamped my mouth closed.

"You didn't say you don't want to sleep with him," she whispered.

My blood was lava coursing through my veins. Why should I deny anything? What business was it of hers? "I already slept with him. This afternoon. In his bed. We *napped*." I returned her hard appraisal. "And I don't think it's his job that you need to prove that you can handle. I think it's me."

I couldn't believe I'd said that. But I'd already jumped off the cliff, there was no climbing back up to the ledge.

"I think you're right. As long as you're in the picture, no woman has a chance to really be with Kieran. You're always there. Your friendship, your intimacies…no one can compete with that. He uses you like a shield so he can hide from any real connection."

I threw up in my mouth a little bit. Just a little bit. She sounded like a bad Cosmo article about unavailable men. "Really? So is this the part where you're convinced that he loves you, but he's just too broken to see it?" I shook my head. "You have to take him the way he is, the same as he has to take you. Don't make excuses for what he does. The way you are together right now? That's the best it's ever going to be."

"You're wrong. He'll let me in when he sees he can trust me."

"Let you in? Oh, for fuck's sake." I hated it when people did that. They'd make every excuse in the world for why someone didn't call, or they didn't connect, or whatever. It had to be because "he's emotionally unavailable." It could never just be because the guy wasn't interested. It was pathetic.

"You know, you're supposed to be his best friend and you act like you don't know him at all."

My mouth opened before I could stop myself. "And you think just because he put his cock in your pussy that you know everything about him. Newsflash: that's just fucking. He didn't make love to you, you didn't have some deeper connection. You asked for the Finn McCool experience, and you got it. That wasn't Kieran. Breakfast the next day? That was Kieran. And you know what's worse? You asked for it like a present. Like something you can buy. And guess what else? It was. Finn McCool *is* for sale, Kieran isn't."

The look in her eyes as something cracked inside of her punched me in the gut. April was my friend. I wasn't supposed to want to hurt her, and I did. I knew my barbs would hit home and I sharpened them anyway. I sliced and cut because I could. That wasn't me. Or at least I didn't want it to be.

"I didn't know any other way to get his attention," she murmured. "He didn't chase me like the other guys do."

I hugged her. "Look, you can fix this."

Why was I trying to help her now? I didn't want to help her, I didn't want them to be together.

But I did want Kieran to be happy.

My selfish heart said that I could make him happy, but I had to take my own advice. If a man wants you, he'll find a way to tell you. And Kieran, in all the years we'd roomed together, had plenty of opportunity to tell me. It wasn't me he'd taken to bed, it was April.

"How?" she asked.

"First, we'll go tonight and we'll sit in the back. He'll know we're there, but we're not going to buy any dances or try to get his attention in any way. But you can't buy any dances from any of the other guys either. Then you'll tell him you need a ride back to the house because we're going to leave your car here. We'll take a cab."

"How are you going to get home?"

"I'll be fine. One of the guys can bring me home." Probably Brant. Or maybe I'd just spend the night on the roof of The Rooster watching the stars and trying not to think about Kieran and April.

She sucked in a deep breath. "I… thank you." April hugged me. "I didn't know I'd feel this way."

Yeah, me either. Instead of answering, I called a cab.

When we got to the club, I put on my party face. I didn't want anyone asking me what was wrong, so it was time to be that girl. The one who was always fun, who always had a slick remark, and who drank like a sailor.

Liquor was the best lube for unwanted social interaction.

We chose a table in the back as I'd suggested and Austin sat down at our table almost immediately. He was, of course, ripped like Adonis. He was wearing a pair of low-slung jeans with a giant belt buckle and nothing else.

He was the one I'd babysat his daughter.

"Hey, honey. Didn't expect you guys back tonight," he said.

"This is as good a place to drink as any," April replied. "Speaking of, I'm going to get some drinks. Rum for you, Claire?"

"Yeah, thanks."

When she was gone, Austin leaned over to whisper in my ear. "Couldn't get enough of Finn McCool, could she?"

I shrugged. "You know how it is."

"I should probably mind my own business, but she knows girls come back here all the time with the same idea she's got."

"She does. But we should both mind our own business." I grinned.

"I meant to ask, this photo shoot we're doing. Can I have copies of all my pics for my portfolio?"

"Oh, of course. And after *Chubbalicious* is making some money, I'll be able to pay you."

"No need. Happy to help." He winked at me. "Although, if you wanted to give me a dollar, I wouldn't mind." The corner of his lip turned up in a smirk as he stood and angled that shiny belt buckle close to my face.

This wasn't usual fare for me. On the nights we came to the club, I didn't usually get dances or put dollars in anyone's jock. I was always Kieran's guest and I hung out in the back sipping my drink and chatting with the girls.

But fuck it, right? That's what they were here for. Maybe all that time I'd spent trying to be different and set apart, I'd been an asshole? I'd been enjoying the scenery without tipping. That was kind of a douche move.

"I guess I owe you one." I pulled a dollar out of my purse and tucked it in the waist of those deliciously worn jeans, my fingers grazing over his oblique.

"Best buck of the night." He winked again.

"Flirt."

"Tease," he tossed back.

"I can't help myself." My tone implied even if I could, I wouldn't.

"Nor should you." He squeezed my shoulder before migrating to another table.

April shoved two shots of rum under my nose. "Did I see what I think I saw? Did you... *tip*?"

I shrugged. "I figured it was time." It grossed me out to realize that I hadn't been tipping not because I thought I was different, but because I didn't want to be that sad, fat girl who had to come to a strip club to put her hands on a man.

Who had to pay for it.

But it wasn't even like that. I knew the guys didn't think of me or any of the women who came to the club that way. The least I could do was cough up a dollar.

Why couldn't epiphanies ever be something that I wanted to deal with? Instead, it was always some stark light of truth on the ugliest, darkest, and saddest parts of myself that I wanted to hide from everyone—including me.

I downed both shots.

"So it's going to be that kind of night?" April asked.

"I work hard. I deserve to have a good time."

"We both do." She waved her arm and one the servers came over. "I don't want to run back to the bar all night. Start me a tab? Bring us six more rum shots and a Manhattan."

She took the Manhattan and gave me the shots.

Another hash mark on the douche scorecard. I'd been so shitty to her and now she was buying my drinks.

"Thanks," I said, sincere.

"Tonight's about having fun, right?"

Except she didn't look like she was having fun. She looked miserable and Kieran wasn't even on the floor yet.

I downed my shots—one right after another.

Sometimes, I was glad for my alcohol tolerance and then other times, I wished I was a lightweight so five dollars would put me in that warm, fuzzy place where everything seemed like a good idea.

FAT

The lights went down and a bachelorette party started shrieking when the routines started. Yeah, I definitely needed those shots.

I was surprised to see Gavin on stage again as the opening act.

April choked on her Manhattan.

"Didn't you see him last night?"

"No. I might have snuck up to the dressing room when you went upstairs." She flashed me a guilty look.

I wouldn't think about what she was doing there. Or who she was doing it with. God, I needed another shot. Something to numb my brain and my heart.

I tried to watch what was going on in front of me. Tried to forget what Gavin said to me, tried to forget what he was like when he was talking and watched him shake his goods, but I wasn't into it. He was pretty, but every time I saw him, I remembered that I was pretty for a fat girl.

I knew I should just let it go. It didn't matter what he thought or what he said. I had to live with myself. He didn't. Maybe I'd buy myself a new dress tomorrow. If I was going to love myself, I should give myself presents, right?

Although, the best present I could give myself right now would be to leave. To go home and take my soon to be drunk ass to bed.

April wandered off, but that didn't surprise me. She was probably trying to find Kieran for some alone time.

It was like that Killers song—I kept seeing every foul thing they could do to each other and it played out like some sick movie in my head. I didn't want to see it, but I couldn't stop.

I'd seen April naked. I knew she didn't have stretch marks, in fact, she had a cute belly button piercing. The bar she wore had a delicate little ladybug on the end. She didn't have any extra fat at all and her boobs would stand up without a bra.

It wasn't hard to picture them together at all. April was just his type. Beautiful people... I slammed back another shot of rum.

I didn't want to even try to picture myself with Kieran, because I wouldn't be able to see anything anyway. I'd want all the lights off.

The room finally started to spin just a little bit, almost like a merry-go-round. And yet, all the fucks I wished I didn't give were still right there in my face.

CHAPTER SEVEN

Saturday morning dawned bright, early, and made me want to puke. It was the day of the shoot and we were all meeting at Longview Lake. The guys were bringing their muscles, their fast cars, and the girls were bringing their fabulous selves.

When I'd conceived of this grand idea, I thought it was the best thing since wide calf boots. But this was going to be my brand, the face I showed to the web and I would stand or fall based on people's impressions of me.

No matter what I said, *Chubbalicious* was me.

I was *Chubbalicious*—in more ways than one.

What was I doing? Why had I ever thought I could do this? Doubt spun like so much sticky, rancid cotton candy and buried my face in the bowl of my hands.

This was utter bullshit. This self-doubt, this fear... Neither of those things were going to help me, so I had to put them out of my head. *Chubbalicious* was what I wanted and I'd never get it if I was afraid to reach for it. I had to trust myself. Especially since I'd already paid the photographer.

Shit, the photographer. It was eight, and Ryan was going to be here in thirty minutes. I'd promised him breakfast. He was a journalism student at the university and the promise of a meal had been more motivation than the small fee I'd paid him.

He'd offered to do it for free, but I believed in paying artists for their work. I couldn't believe how many people had asked me to design clothes for them and tell me that my payment would be exposure, that I could put it in my portfolio.

Seriously? Fuck you.

I didn't mind working for trade, but in my mind, exposure isn't trade. Hollie was the writer and she'd written the descriptive copy for all of the pieces. I'd given her two of the dresses she was going to model. One for doing the shoot, and another for writing the copy. Rosa was doing makeup and hair, so she got two dresses as well.

And Ryan Wells, I'd paid him less than he was worth, so I was more than happy to feed him.

I pulled out the v-neck stretch tee I'd planned on wearing. It was ridiculously pink, but it read *I Am Chubbalicious*. The v dipped down right between the double b, which I found endlessly funny because there was nothing b about this shirt—it was all double d.

I shimmied into a pair of distressed jeans and low-heeled gladiator sandals and called it good.

The bell rang and I peered out the window to see that Ryan Wells was right on time. But he most certainly did not look like any journalism student I'd ever met. He was the same size as Kieran—tall, broad shouldered, looked like a football player.

I paused mid-thought. If I wanted people to stop thinking in stereotypes, I had to do it too. It wasn't even something I realized I did. But why couldn't a guy who was into photography and journalism be into taking care of his body?

Because I'm a psycho. I sighed as I opened the door. Sometimes, I thought that I made a bigger deal out of it than anyone else.

"Hey, I'm running behind. Breakfast will be a little late." I apologized and hoped he wasn't too unhappy with that development.

He grinned. "That's a relief. I was working on a project for Ancient Civ all night and I might've just eaten a whole pizza. So no worries. We can get straight to the shoot."

"Fabulous! Let me grab my bag. Everyone is going to meet us there." I reached over to the table. "I have the model releases and paperwork here." It was in a shiny new pink folder that had been embossed with *Chubbalicious.*

When I'd started this last year, I'd been very concerned with branding, with swag, and I'd spent a lot of money of it. But I'd learned that no matter how good your swag, your branding, you still needed a good product. I should've developed the product first. And now I had all of these *Chubbalicious* office supplies, stationary, note pads, pens... Oh, the pens.

He accepted it and held the door wider for me to exit.

I kind of thought we'd ride with Kieran, but his car wasn't in the driveway. I hope he didn't flake on me. If he did, I'd never forgive him.

Or April, if he was with her. They both knew how important this was to me.

I knew that was totally selfish, but I didn't generally ask my friends for things. I asked Kieran not to fuck my other friends and that was about it. Except for *Chubbalicious*. It was my fatted calf, my golden god, my temple and my priest. It was everything.

"Are you nervous? Don't be." He answered his own question before I could. "You're going to be great."

"Me? I'm worried about the clothes."

He raised a brow. "Everyone is nervous in front of the camera, and you're still doing a couple publicity shots, right?"

"I don't know if all that's necessary." I opened my car door and slid into the driver's seat. It was nothing so nice as what all the guys drove. It was a newer Chevy Impala. Practical and dependable.

"Yes, it definitely is." He flashed a grin. "You'll love them. I promise."

Pictures of myself? Looking at them was kind of like a guiding tour in hell. I knew I had a pretty face, but I didn't photograph well—and that had nothing to do with being fat. Even when I was a kid, before puberty, boobs, hormones, and my body rebelling against me, I still despised pictures of myself.

"If you can make me like pictures of myself—" I paused. "—well, the thought's so foreign I really don't know what I'd do."

"Let me take more and show them to all your friends, so they'll book me. That's what you'll do." He smiled wider. "Or that's what I'd appreciate you doing."

"You got it, doll."

We chatted about music, photography, and even football on the way to Longview.

Everyone was there when we arrived. "How did you guys beat me here?" My voice might have warbled a little, thick with emotion. They knew how important this was and they came.

I think part of me expected them to bail, to let me down.

Why was I friends with these people if I didn't think I could count on them or trust them to believe in me?

Another goddamn epiphany slapped me so hard I almost fell over.

It wasn't just them—it was me. I didn't believe in me either.

You know Claire, if you'd just trim up a bit, it would be easier for people to get to know you. You'd have so many more friends. My mother's voice echoed in my head.

I never understood what she meant by that—that somehow the shape of my body prevented people from knowing me. And if it did, I said I didn't want those friends anyway.

You'll never keep a man if you don't get your weight under control.

"Shut up," I muttered. Her "helpful" voice on a loop was as bad as my own. Why did it always have to come back to this? I plastered a smile on my face and joined the group.

"Thank you all so much for coming. It really means the world to me."

Seeing Rosa and Hollie in the dresses I'd made—how utterly fucking fabulous they looked—it touched me deeper than any stupid voice on any lame loop. This was what I was meant to do and I was good at it.

My eyes watered when they hugged me, stupid pollen. Because I wasn't the type to snivel or cry over something like this. It had to be the pollen.

"You guys are perfect," I said after I broke the hug.

Rosa spun in a circle, the crinoline under the skirt swung out to reveal more leg. "I kind of do look perfect, don't I? I feel like a rockabilly princess."

"Am I still up first?" Kieran said.

I nodded. "Hell yeah. You and Rosa, like we talked about."

He grinned and pulled off his shirt. I tried not to look, but Rosa didn't make any such effort.

"It's good to be me," she said.

Hollie laughed. "No kidding."

My gaze was drawn to Brant, and he smiled. It wasn't a sly smirk, or even a naughty grin. It was a genuine smile. My lips curved of their own accord. There was something about the expression on his face, like maybe he was proud of me.

Not like I was a puppy who'd done something cute and should be indulged, but actually proud of me.

Something foreign swelled in my chest. *Thank you*, I mouthed.

Always, he mouthed back.

I turned my attention back to the scene in front of me and Ryan had already started snapping pictures.

Kieran lifted Rosa up to sit on the hood of his Challenger and he crouched down in front of her so that Rosa could lean forward and brace her hands on his shoulders. His very broad shoulders. I tried not to drool. The shot wouldn't do much for the dress, but I'd planned to use a series of pictures and a big splash page for each item. Risky, with what I knew about people's clicking/buying habits, but there was a certain feel that I wanted to capture for each thing. Something I wanted to transmit to the consumer and I wanted them to feel beautiful in my clothes.

Basically, if you buy this dress, you can have anything you want. Not just any man, but the world. Yourself.

Maybe that was ambitious for some fabric and thread to accomplish, but I wanted to try.

Kieran swept her up in his arms and then proceeded to lift her over his head. She squealed. "Don't squirm and you'll be fine. Claire, come fix these ruffles."

The pose was like all those vintage muscle beach guys holding the woman above their heads. Only it was for *Chubbalicious* and the woman wasn't a size five. She was a 22/24.

I rushed in to smooth the skirt and let it fall over Kieran's shoulder. Part of me wanted to take a while, not only to be closer to Kieran, but to see how long he could hold her up. He wasn't even straining. This was nothing to him.

I looked around to see if anyone could tell that my panties had just melted off of me.

"You sure you're okay?" Rosa asked, biting her lip.

Kieran started to lower his arms, playing at fatigue and when she shrieked, he hoisted her aloft again, laughing. "Come on, lass. I bench my own body weight and I definitely weigh more than you. Relax."

I arched a brow. "That wasn't nice."

"You're next."

"Oh, I think not." No, I could never let that happen. "And you just ruined all my work." I fussed with the skirt again, maybe longer than I needed to.

"You like feeling me up anyway."

Caught, my face flamed, but I lifted my chin. "Well, who wouldn't?"

Rosa giggled. "Stop feeling up Muscles McIrish here. I wanna turn."

"You're so bad." Hollie laughed from the sideline. "But uh, yeah. I get a turn, too."

"Ladies, there's enough muscle to go around," Austin said and tipped his cowboy hat.

Kieran shrugged. "It's the Oirish."

I realized that Ryan hadn't stopped snapping. The film kept rolling through all of this. It might be good to have some candid outtakes, but I certainly didn't want a picture of my ass in the shot.

I eyed Kieran critically, forgetting that he was my hottie roommate. He was advertising. I unsnapped the button on his jeans and tugged them down an inch to better show off his obliques—or as April liked to call it, his Adonis apron.

He didn't move a single muscle or react in any way. Except the look in his eyes. For some reason I couldn't explain, I had to look up at him. It was like the tide and I'd have had an easier time turning it than avoiding his stare.

It was hot, hungry, but it couldn't possibly be for me. Could it?

"That's better." I mumbled.

"Is it?" he asked, as if we were talking about something so banal as the weather, rather than me almost ripping his jeans off him.

"If that's part of the treatment, I'm glad I signed up," Brant said.

"Whatever. You know you'll get that anyway," Austin teased.

"Will he?" Kieran asked.

I pretended I didn't hear him and walked out of the shot. Ryan kept snapping.

They moved through several other poses and dresses. The rest of the shoot went smoothly. It was obvious from the way everyone interacted, that they were having a good time.

Even when April showed up carrying two large picnic baskets. I didn't know if I was glad to see her or not.

She hugged me tight. "I wanted to help. I hope it's okay."

What was I going to say to that? I didn't even know how I felt about it. April had been one of my best friends, I thought. Until lately, when I really started thinking about some of the things she said to me.

Part of me didn't believe that she was here to help. She was here for Kieran.

But what did that matter in the scheme of things? If he wanted to be with her, he would. There was nothing I, or anyone else could or should do about that.

So I hugged her back. "Thanks. That's great. I'm sure everyone is getting hungry. I promised Ryan here breakfast." I nodded to the photographer.

She beamed. "Great. When's break time?"

Rosa pursed her lips. "Who invited the skinny girl? This is a fat girl only party."

I thought about how it would feel if it was the other way around. *This is a skinny girl only party.* I knew she was teasing, but it wasn't okay either.

I put my arm around her. "This is a gorgeous girl party."

"You bet it is," Brant said from where he was already rummaging through the baskets.

"There's some beers in the trunk. And some soda," April called to him.

"You're the best," he answered.

"So you know, Claire still hasn't had her turn," Kieran said.

"Oh!" Hollie exclaimed. "Come on, Rosa. We need to get her hair and makeup."

"I really don't think—"

"You promised us. Me and Brant." Kieran reminded me.

"It's a waste of everyone's time. I'm not going to use them."

"You're not getting out of it, Claire." Ryan grinned. "Remember? For my portfolio?"

I looked around at all of the expectant faces. "Fine." Just because I agreed to do it didn't mean I actually had to look at them.

CHAPTER EIGHT

After Hollie and Rosa finished pasting on eyelashes, makeup, and doing my hair, I stood in front of the Challenger and eyed it suspiciously.

They wanted me on the hood.

Not a fucking chance.

It just didn't look that sturdy.

And if I dented it, I would die of utter and absolute humiliation.

No, no, and much more no.

"Yes, Claire." It was as if Kieran could hear my thoughts. "I sit on it all the time."

I shook my head without speaking.

"It's reinforced. Special modification for that custom engine. Come on, baby."

He called me baby.

I shook my head again, but this time it was more like a maraca. Maybe that would rattle those stupid thoughts out of my head.

April came to my rescue. "Here, use the blanket." She spread out the red and white checkered blanket in front of the car.

"Yes!" I latched on to that idea.

"Oh, this is good. I like the contrast of colors." Ryan motioned for me to get with the program.

I found myself being led to the blanket by both Brandt and Kieran.

"Wait, first shot let's do all three with Claire. Sit down with your knees crossed. Then Claire, you're going to lay across their laps," Ryan directed.

I followed his directions. Everyone was so set on this course, so why the fuck not?

"Damn it, Austin. Your belt buckle is killing me," I grumped.

"That's not my belt buckle, sweetheart."

My eyes went wide and the shutter kept clicking away.

"That's it. That expression. Put your finger against your lips. Pin up style… faux startled. You know what I mean."

I knew exactly what he meant, but I wasn't a pin up sex kitten.

"Look at me. It's just a camera, and I'm behind it, right?" He peered out from around the lens. It's just me looking at you."

He was right. The camera wasn't some raging beast that was trying to hurt me, or wound me. It was just him. Looking at me while I was wrapped in male stripper.

I tittered.

"There you go." His face was once again consumed by the shuttered mons—camera and I started to relax. "Okay, now I want just Brant and Kieran."

"Fine," Austin huffed in faux indignation, but grinned. "That was too much sausage for me anyway." He put one arm around Rosa and the other around Hollie.

I laughed.

Ryan continued to push us through a series of poses, each a bit more risqué than the last. I tried not to think about it—being pressed between them. They were both so strong and hard, a contrast to my softness.

Soon, I couldn't tell who touched me where. It was all sensation—heat. And when I surrendered to it, everything changed. It was like turning on a light.

"There it is, that's what I want." Ryan praised me.

"You like this?" Brant whispered.

"We do," Kieran said in my other ear.

They were trying to kill me.

In fact, I was sure I was dead. This was either heaven or hell, I didn't know which. Maybe both.

"Now, just Kieran," Ryan ordered.

This was supposed to be my shoot, but instead, it had turned into Ryan's and I couldn't find the wherewithal to care.

My limbs were pliable—boneless. I don't think I could've stood on my own if I wanted to.

Kieran lifted me easily and I found myself on the hood of that damned car. He was posing me, moving me as he pleased and I let him. His hands were in my hair, sliding down my sides...

"Look at me, that's right," Ryan said.

Kieran positioned himself between my thighs and my self-respect was this tiny voice in the back of my head shrieking that everyone could see. But primal brain didn't care. Primal brain just wanted Kieran to keep touching.

Kieran leaned into my neck, his breath teased the shell of my ear. "Tonight, you're going to bring Brant home, and I know you're going to fuck him."

My lips parted and I gasped.

The shutter continued to snap away, capturing every moment as stark as any memory.

"But I'm not bringing April home. I'm going to be in my room, alone."

I tightened my grip on his shoulders, as if that would make him stop talking. Whatever he said next, I couldn't unhear, no matter what that meant for us.

For me.

For all of it.

He took my nails digging into his shoulders as tacit permission. "I'll be listening to every sound that comes through those walls. Every gasp, every cry."

Rather than looking at the camera now, I found myself watching Brant. I don't know what I expected to see there, but it wasn't the blatant arousal I recognized from our night together.

I clung tighter.

"Jesus, every woman on the planet is going to order something from *Chubbalicious* if it turns them into Claire," Rosa half-whispered.

They were all watching me, rapt, but it seemed like they were so far away. Like another dimension, even April.

"—And I'm going to come in my hand wishing it was me."

His words broke the spell. I shoved hard against his shoulders and he released me.

"Show's over." I hopped off the car and smoothed my hair.

"Those were some great shots. I can't wait to show them to you," Ryan said.

I couldn't believe how calm he was, like Kieran hadn't almost fucked me right there on the car. I took a deep, calming breath. Okay, so maybe he hadn't almost fucked me, but it was creeping on carnal knowledge.

Why would he say that to me?

I bit the inside of my cheek hard when I tried to talk. It made me feel stupid, but it was probably a sign from the universe to just keep my mouth closed.

Now that imagery of Kieran, it would be in my head forever—of him alone in his room, stroking himself… I shivered.

I didn't know what he was playing at, but we'd have to have that shit out directly. He couldn't say those things to me, it wasn't fair. Not unless he meant them.

Hell, what did it matter if he meant them? We'd never even so much as kissed and now he was telling me he was jerking off thinking about me? I wasn't sure if I was flattered or offended. Maybe a little of both.

"Claire—"

I turned to look at him, he still had his shirt off, his jeans unbuttoned. My mouth went dry. "Who am I talking to? Kieran or Finn McCool?"

My words hit him hard as any fist.

"What's wrong, Claire?" April asked.

"Nothing." I shook my head. I didn't want everyone to know I was having a fucking meltdown because things got a little heated. "Thanks for doing the shoot, Kieran. I appreciate it."

His mask was in place again. "Anytime, sweetheart."

Yeah, that wasn't Kieran. That was Finn.

And that hurt, because anyone could have Finn. Anyone could buy him. Kieran was supposed to be mine.

There was my problem in a nutshell. He wasn't mine, and I'd started to think of him like he was. Even if we were together, he still wasn't mine, you can't own another person—and who would want to?

I sighed.

"Thanks, everyone. I've got to drop off our intrepid photographer, so I'm going to head out."

Brant met me at the car. Ryan didn't wait for me to say anything, he just got in and closed the door, giving us a modicum of privacy.

"What was that about?"

"I can't even." I shook my head. How was I supposed to tell him even if I were so inclined?

He hugged me. "I'll meet you at your house and we'll go grab dinner like we planned."

His arms were warm, safe, and the comfort I found there had nothing to do with height, muscle or anything but the man who embraced me.

"I'll change."

"I kind of like your pin up couture."

"Okay then. I'll wear it. Even these eyelashes."

He released me and opened the door for me. I slid into the seat and started the car.

"It's none of my business, but that's not the guy I expected you to be dating." Ryan said.

"We're not really dating." We hadn't put a label on what we were doing and I liked it that way.

"You and that other guy, I thought my camera was going to explode. You're on fire together."

"Are we?" I asked, curious now how everyone else saw our interaction.

"You were great models. The chemistry was explosive. It's like that other girl said. If you use these pictures, every woman will wish she was you."

I could tell that he genuinely meant what he said, but I didn't see it. It was unimaginable.

Just as I put the car into gear, April put her arms around Kieran. He returned the embrace, but watched me over the top of her head.

I drove as fast as my little Chevy would carry us away from Kieran and everything he stirred in me.

FAT

CHAPTER NINE

Brant was sitting with his back against his car door waiting for me when I got to the house—Kieran's car was nowhere to be found.

So much for staying in tonight alone. I knew he had to work, but that's why I expected him home. He napped after we watched *American Horror Story*. Although, to be fair, I'd made plans with Brant.

My brain wouldn't stop picturing him doing…things. But now instead of him by himself, thinking about me, my stupid imagination had painted April into the scene. He was touching her, tasting her—she was making those damn sounds like she had the night of her birthday.

Maybe I should just fuck him for my birthday present too. After all, it was just Finn McCool. He'd do it.

Even having the thought broke my heart.

"What's wrong? And don't try to bullshit me and say there's nothing wrong. What did Kieran do?" Brant said when he saw my expression.

I searched Brant's face for some ulterior motive. There was only concern. "He's just being a douche." I slid down to sit next to him.

"He's jealous."

"What?"

"You're spending all of your time with me or *Chubbalicious*, and that's new. You've always been his."

"But he set us up. That makes no sense to me." Who was I trying to convince? Him or me?

"He'll get over it. Or not. And you'll stop seeing me to be with him."

I turned my head sharply.

"If you think no one saw the burn between you two, you're sadly mistaken. If you don't want to talk about it, that's fine. But don't lie and say it's not there."

The part of me that was a selfish bitch wanted to tell him everything, because now with this rift with April, Brant was quickly becoming my best friend. I could feel the pieces clicking into place. I wanted to tell him things, wanted his thoughts and his advice.

Most of all, I didn't want to hurt him.

"No," I said slowly. "I won't deny it. I guess there *is* no denying it." I took a deep breath. "How do you feel about that?"

"I guess it depends on what you want to do. If you want me to be your friend, I can be your friend, Claire. That's why I wanted to wait before we had sex. I want you, there's no refuting that. But what am I going to say here? That it's fine? It's not. It'll hurt like a motherfucker." His laugh was self-deprecating. "Will I respect what you want? Of course."

"Do you want to keep seeing me?"

"I thought that was clear."

"Obviously, we have chemistry too." We did, because the way he touched me—it was the best sex I'd ever had.

"If we're being honest, we all had chemistry together."

My eyes widened as his implication became clear.

"Shocked? You shouldn't be. You make jokes about it all the time."

"Only because it's a dirty fantasy." I pursed my lips, trying to hold back whatever else my mouth could say without my brain's permission.

"It doesn't have to be. Kieran and I have shared women before. You want him. I still want you." His tone was matter of fact. "And if I'm not mistaken, you want us both."

I didn't think my whole body could blush, but I had to be because I was hot everywhere. I'd never thought of myself as a prude, but maybe I was. The woman I wanted to be would've grabbed this opportunity by the balls and shook them like maracas.

Except the woman I was? Not so much.

I laughed. It was an awkward, tinny sound. "If I'm embarrassed to be naked in front of one man, what would I do with two?"

"Come so hard you see stars. Now tell me what he did to piss you off."

This wasn't happening. It just wasn't. Synapses refused to connect and fire. He'd basically told me that I could have everything I wanted. I could live a fantasy. "But I don't want the guys who work at The Rooster. I want you, Brant. The real you. The one I connect with. I don't want Finn McCool. I want Kieran. Your bodies are gorgeous, that's not in question. But I want more than that."

"You've got it. At least from me."

"I don't have it from Kieran. I did, until things got weird. Now, he's Finn." I slumped. "Shit, I sound like a total psycho."

"No, he does. Switching back and forth between personalities? We call that multiple personality disorder." Brant grinned.

I just love you was on the tip of my tongue. He made me laugh, he made feel safe, he seemed to know how to make everything right. What wasn't to love? But I wasn't in love with him. I said I love you to Kieran all the time, to Rosa, to Hollie, to April.

But Brant was different. He wouldn't hear it the same way.

I was glad my tongue obeyed me with that little tidbit. Instead, I said, "Thanks."

"For what? Offering to bang you and your crush?"

I giggled. "For being you. For making being me okay."

Surprise bloomed on his face. "Why would it not be okay?"

"You're always so sure of yourself."

"Usually, but if you held out on me any longer before you said yes, you might have changed all that," he teased me. "Can we go eat now? I'm starving."

"You just stuffed your face with April's picnic."

"That sounded way dirtier than it was."

I laughed and nudged his shoulder. "You know what I mean."

"I only had one sandwich and some strawberries. I need some protein if I'm going to work out later."

"You work out before you dance?"

"Yeah. Makes everything *harder*."

"Everything?"

"Everything. Wanna see?" he teased me.

"Maybe I just do." I reached over and grabbed his biceps. He flexed for me and that made me giggle too. It was silly, but it was nice to have this freedom to touch and be touched.

I guess it was more than a freedom, it was a kind of intimacy. An intimacy that would most likely be ruined if I took him up on his offer.

Even though I knew some things were better left as fantasy, now that the idea had taken root in my brain, I couldn't stop thinking about it. Remembering what it was like being pressed between them at the shoot earlier—he'd said I could have that again. I could have everything. I tried to push it out of my head.

He took my hand from his arm and pulled it down over his chest slowly. Down to his abs, down further to the waist of his jeans. I recognized the move from the club. All the guys did that when they were giving dances.

I hated that I knew that and I hated that it bothered me.

How many times did I need him to prove I was special to him? My brain knew that I was, but my heart was afraid to believe it.

But I didn't stop touching him. I should have. For a million reasons. Because I wasn't in the right place to have a relationship, I had feelings for Kieran, and I didn't know what I wanted from Brant. I was officially an asshole.

Yet, Brant didn't seem to mind.

"What if I did… this?" I drew my hand down further over and played with the pull on his zipper.

"So what if you did?" He grinned. "You can do anything you want."

This time, it was *me* who leaned over and kissed *him*. He tasted like strawberries.

Brant pulled me across his lap so I straddled him. This wasn't normally a position I enjoyed—it always made me feel so big and awkward, like a drunken yak. But it felt too good for me to worry about it.

Even though I was on top, he was still very much in control. His hands were under my shirt, cupping my breasts—I'd swear he had extra limbs if I hadn't seen him naked. It seemed he could touch me everywhere at once.

He moved from my mouth to my neck, biting and licking, and I braced my hands on his shoulders.

God, we were making out like teenagers in the driveway. "What if someone sees us?" I panted.

"Let them watch and wish they were you." He grasped my hips and pulled me harder against him, grinding us into each other.

Just like everything else with Brant, it felt too good to stop. His Mustang hid us from the road, and the bushes would probably block the neighbor's view. Probably. But with the pleasure building, I didn't care.

I could've done any number of things. Suggested we go inside, dragged him into the backseat of his car, anything but what I did.

Because just as Brant brought me off, Kieran pulled into the driveway behind Brant's car.

Our eyes met, and I knew I was making my "O" face.

But I didn't look away and I sure as hell didn't tell Brant to stop.

Kieran didn't look away either.

Those seconds seemed to last for years. I drowned in bliss, and Kieran. Except when the storm passed, I looked away, embarrassed.

"Shit. Kieran's back." I straightened my clothes.

"It's not like he's your dad."

I scrambled to my feet. "No, but…he saw me."

"So?"

"Brant! Can we just go? Please?"

"Yeah." He got to his feet. "Where do you want to go?"

"Wherever."

"You should at least say goodbye," he said after he stood.

"Why?" No, there was no reason for that.

"Because April is in the car with him."

It shouldn't have felt like getting kicked in the gut, but it did. What did it matter that April came back with him? I was dry-humping in the driveway with his co-worker.

"Did we interrupt something?" April asked when she got out of the car.

I looked back and forth between Kieran and Brant. Kieran looked like a storm cloud and Brant seemed very pleased with himself.

"No. We were done. We're heading to Roadhouse for some steak."

April slid a sideways glance to Kieran. "Steak sounds really good."

I knew the polite thing to do would be to invite her—them, but I didn't want to.

"You guys can come if you want," Brant said.

"I'm actually kind of tired," Kieran answered, his eyes never leaving my face. "You guys go. I'll catch a nap."

I swallowed hard, unable to remember why what he'd said had made me so angry to begin with. "Don't watch AHS without me."

He smiled then, but it was a slow, sad sort of expression. "Never."

"April and I can run to Roadhouse and get carryout," Brant offered.

I was starting to think he was the devil.

"Would you? Man, that sounds great," Kieran said.

"I—" April broke off.

"You can help carry." He opened the passenger door before sliding in the driver's seat. "Come here," he said to me.

I leaned over and stuck my head through the window. "What?"

"Fix your shit." He kissed me and then whispered in my ear again. "Whether you want to fuck us both or not is irrelevant. You guys have baggage from earlier. Get rid of it. For all our sakes, okay?"

He was right. I needed to be a grown up, which really wasn't anywhere near as cool as it was cracked up to be. "Yeah," I agreed. "And uh, bring me some of those rolls with the honey cinnamon butter."

"You got it, gorgeous." He winked.

And it reminded me of April's party at The Rooster, when Kieran winked at me and my life as I knew it was launched on its ass.

April got in the car reluctantly and mouthed *"We need to talk."*

Probably, but I didn't want to.

What could I say to her, anyway? I certainly didn't want to hear what she had to say.

Brant pulled out of the driveway before I could say anything anyway.

Suddenly I felt naked and exposed.

I didn't want to be alone with him because it meant facing that we'd crossed a line. I knew we'd crossed it, but if neither of us acknowledged it aloud, maybe we could uncross it. Or at least ignore it until things were back to normal.

I wanted them to be normal, right? Because maybe Kieran was a fantasy best left as the path I didn't take. What if I fell in love with him, and I was just another notch on Finn McCool's bedpost?

Or what if I was the pity fuck? That was even worse. I imagined him closing his eyes while he was on top of me and thinking about god and country so I didn't kick him out.

How could I be so stupid?

"Do you want to start, or should I?" he said.

I closed my eyes, as if not looking at him could somehow drown out the cacophony in my head and all the things he was going to say that I didn't want to hear.

"You."

"Will you at least look at me, Claire?"

"I can't."

"Why not?"

I took a deep breath to steady myself. "I'm afraid of what I'll see."

"You didn't mind looking at me earlier when you were grinding on Brant."

"That's not fair. I didn't expect you home."

"Neither did you bother to stop."

"Would you have?" My eyes were still closed.

"Not a chance."

"Well, then." What else could I say to that?

"Claire, look at me."

The pads of his fingertips were warm on my jaw and he tilted my face up and my eyelashes fluttered—eyes opening against my better judgment.

"Was that so hard?" His voice was gentle.

"Yes." My stupid lip quivered.

"I'm sorry."

That wasn't what I expected. "For what?"

"For earlier. I shouldn't have said that to you. Can you forgive me and we'll forget about it and move on?"

This was what I thought I wanted, but it couldn't be that easy. Not for me, anyway. I'd pick it to death forever unless there was some real resolution. "It wasn't what you said. It was that it was Finn saying it and not you."

"Finn is me."

"Is he? Because all this time, I thought Kieran was someone else. I thought Finn was a character you made up, and you get to play at being him."

His shoulders sagged. "That's because I wanted you to think I'm a better man than I am."

I was torn. His words cut me, but they pissed me off too. I was pissed for him, pissed that he'd lied to me...only, those moments of quiet that were just us, that afternoon I'd spent in his arms, that wasn't a lie. That was real.

"You just broke my heart," I whispered. "You made me think that our friendship was special. That it was something different."

"So did you. How do you think it felt to realize that you weren't just watching the show, but me. *Me!*" he snarled. "And then you left with Brant anyway."

"You wanted me to!" He'd set me up with him, for fuck's sake.

"No, Claire. That changed everything."

"What did?" I didn't understand.

"The way you watched me." He pushed his hand through his hair. "I always thought I was more to you than pretty meat. That's all this is." He pointed down at his body. "It's just meat. It doesn't matter. We were more."

"And less."

"And less," he repeated quietly.

"It was just a dance."

"But it gave me hope that you finally saw something more in me. It killed me that you saw me like everyone else, but it meant maybe things would go to the next level."

"Why didn't you tell me that's what you wanted?" I cried.

"Because I figured if you wanted me, you'd say so."

"That's what I thought about you."

"I don't think you realize how everyone else sees you, Claire. You're like this force of nature. You don't ever scale a mountain in your path, you barrel through it and no one is going to stop you."

I laughed. "I thought out of everyone, you'd see through my hype. That's all it is. I'm faking it until I make it, Kieran. I'd never in a million years think a guy like you could want anything from me but friendship."

"We're a fekking pair, aren't we?"

"Can this be fixed?" I asked.

"Call Brant and tell him you're not hungry and that he should take April home." His eyes were dark and full of promise.

In that second, if I said yes, I could have him. I could have Kieran Holt. But at Brant's expense. I couldn't hurt him like that.

"I can't do that."

"Can't? You mean you won't." His words were practically a growl.

"No, Kieran. I won't. I won't call someone I made plans with, someone who is currently buying all of us steak dinners, and tell him that he just spent a hundred dollars for no reason so you can get your dick wet."

"Is that all you think of me?"

I sighed. "No. Of course not. It's just, we haven't hashed anything out. All we did was acknowledge that we're attracted to each other. And you're seeing April now. Whether or not that's what you intended. You said you were coming home alone tonight." I didn't mean for it to sound like a reprimand, but it did.

"This isn't tonight, is it?" he answered.

"That's what I mean. You'd never be content with just one woman."

"You like fucking Brant," he shot back.

"Of course I do. Jesus, what's not to like? He tells me I'm beautiful, tells me I can have anything in the world that I want, and then proceeds to give it to me. And only me."

"Are you sure about that?"

"Really?" I growled. "Did you just say that to me? You're the one who set me up with him. If he was a douche, why would you do that? Or are you just sowing conflict where there was none?"

He grabbed my shoulders. "I just don't understand why, after two dates, you'd be so quick to trust him." He looked away and down at his feet. "And me, after five years, you don't."

"In all the time I've known you, you've never had a committed relationship."

"Yes, I have. With you."

I hated that his words made me warm. They shouldn't have. "So then what was that conga line of women through your room?"

"They meant nothing to me."

"So why would give your body to someone who meant nothing to you?"

"You don't understand."

"No, Kieran. I don't." I shook my head.

"This is it then? You're picking Brant?"

Fear knifed me. I wasn't ready for the possibility of us to be over. I'd only just realized it was something that could happen. "I'm not picking anyone. Brant and I—" I didn't know what we were and I didn't know how to define it to Kieran. "—I'm not going to treat him badly, Kieran. Not even for you."

"What *would* you do for me?" he demanded. "I offered to stop seeing April."

"But I didn't ask you to and I'd never ask you to be shitty to her."

"Maybe you should. Don't you want to know how far I'll go for you? You said Brant offered you the world. What was his quest?" I couldn't tell if he was being sarcastic or not.

I bit my lip and the sound of my heartbeat thundered in my ears like crashing waves. "You."

"I'm not sure I understand." He cocked his head to the side.

Jesus, but he was beautiful. I couldn't believe I was standing here, having this conversation with him. The hard line of his jaw, the sullen, bad boy set to his mouth, the way his hair swept over his forehead as if it too had something to rebel against.

"He said that the three of us had chemistry together," I blurted. I hoped he understood the implication, I wasn't ready to say it out loud.

He blinked owlishly. "Seriously?"

Kieran seemed surprised. "Yeah."

"Is that what you want?"

"I don't know what I want. I mean… there's you." I shrugged.

"Yeah, me. I'm nothing special, lass."

"Have you looked at yourself?"

"Every day." He shoved his hands in his pockets. "So what's supposed to happen here? Did he leave so we could get started? This isn't a porno."

I giggled, but it wasn't really funny. "No. He told me to sort my shit and I'm trying."

"Is it sorted then?"

"I don't think so."

"I love you, Claire."

If anything he'd said before hit me hard, this was a fucking freight train. He loved me, but was he *in love* with me?

"I love you, too."

"Then how is Brant even part of the equation?"

"Because I'm afraid."

He cupped my jaw. "Of what, me?"

No, of me. Of my own failure. Of my own faults. He was just too everything. He was too beautiful, too perfect. He was like the sun and he'd burn me if I got too close, or even stared too long. "You can have any woman you want. So could Brant." I exhaled, and before I could rethink my word choice, I said, "I've got a pretty face, but—"

"But nothing." He yanked me against him hard. "Do you feel that?"

Oh, I did. I felt his arousal pressed against me and I almost didn't believe it. "Yes."

"Who do you think that's for?"

This was everything I wanted, so why was I holding back? Brant knew I wanted Kieran. I'd told him. I'd told him I didn't want anything serious as well. So what stopped me?

"I still don't believe it's real."

"You're happy enough with Brant."

"I guess because he's not perfect. Like me. We're not "traditionally attractive" as some people like to say."

"Who the fuck says that? There are all sorts of women all over Brant and you've always got men looking at you. Maybe you're not a size two, but who says you have to be?"

I had a prepared rant about societal expectations, advertising, fat-shaming… but it wasn't any of those things. It was me. I didn't actually believe I was beautiful. Not deep down.

"Me." I hated how small and sad I sounded. So pathetic.

His mouth slammed into mine—it was like guerrilla kissing. But it was absolutely everything I'd dreamed it could be.

He made me feel tiny, delicate, and treasured. His mouth was so hard and commanded the kiss like some kind of general. My arms twined around his neck and I couldn't help thinking he tasted of sweet mint.

And I remembered April carried these super sweet mints her purse. She liked to use them after giving oral.

I broke the kiss and jerked away from him.

"What the hell, Claire?" He looked stunned, his voice was ragged.

"I can't, I just can't."

I fled to my room and slammed the door. I curled up in the middle of my bed waiting for the knock that never came.

FAT

CHAPTER TEN

"Claire, it's me." Brant said through the door some time later.

"Come in."

He had two plastic containers from Roadhouse.

"What happened? I thought you were going to talk to him?"

"Is he here?"

"No, he's gone. April called a cab." He shrugged. "I offered to take her home, but she was really upset and wouldn't even wait inside."

"I should go talk to her." I wrapped my arms even more tightly around my knees. I didn't want to talk to her. For a little bit, I just wanted something to be about me.

"That's probably the last thing you should do. Because like I said, everyone saw what was between you and Kieran today. Including April."

I sighed. "Why did he do this?"

"Do you want the honest answer or the answer that will make you feel better?"

I pursed my lips. "Honestly? Neither."

"What about your steak? You want that?" He pushed it at me on the bed.

"Yes, yes I do."

"I have to leave in a little while. I need to hit the gym and get ready for work. Are you going to be okay?"

"You are unbelievable. Really. Where is your shining armor? Because I swear you have it."

"It's not shining. It's red. It's the armor and the noble steed." He brushed his lips against mine—his kiss so different from Kieran's. "Don't change the subject. Are you okay? If you don't want to talk about what happened, that's fine, but I need to know that you're good."

I nodded. "I'm good. And so are you, much too good to me."

"You've said that before. Don't you think you deserve to be treated well?"

"There's treating me well and then there's you." I laughed.

"And when it's time to choose, I hope you remember that."

If anyone else had said that to me, I'd have felt pressure. Like he was only being nice to me to get something out of me, but I already knew Brant wasn't that kind of person and it made me feel like an asshole that I couldn't just forget about Kieran.

But things like this didn't happen to girls like me.

It was rare to have one man interested, let alone two.

As soon as I had that thought, I wanted to rip it out of my head. How dare I think so lowly of myself? As if all that defined my value as a person was if someone wanted to fuck me?

I was just as bad as everyone else. No, I was worse. Because I put on this face, but it was a lie.

And I was going to hurt someone who didn't deserve it.

If Kieran and I were meant to be, it would have happened a long time before now. I needed to put him out of my head.

"Will you come by after work tonight?" I asked Brant.

"You know, there's not much to go do when I get off work." He teased.

"I don't want to go out. I want to stay in. All night."

"Oh really?" His grin was adorable and just a little panty-melting. I don't know why I'd never noticed that all the times before he'd asked me out.

"Yeah, really." I grabbed his shirt and pulled him toward me for another kiss.

This was good. Brant was good. If I could just stop being a silly bitch, I could be happy.

"Are you sure?"

"Let me show you how sure." My hands went to the waist of his jeans.

"Your steak is going to be cold."

"It'll still be good. After." I sank to my knees on the carpet and tugged his jeans down to his knees.

He'd gone commando.

Brant's eyes were dark, glittering with desire and his cock was hard enough to drive nails. I wanted him inside me, but this wasn't about me. It was about him. I wanted to make him feel all the things he'd done for me. I wanted to give him pleasure with no expectation of anything in return—ecstasy just for the sake of itself.

He allowed me to do as I wished with him, his eyes on my every move, but he kept his palms flat on the bed.

When I'd taken him into my mouth, he whispered a trespass. "What would you do right now if Kieran was here?"

I pulled back from my work. "This isn't for Kieran. It's for you. And he's not here. Let's not talk about this anymore."

"What if I told you he was watching us?"

"What if you're just being perverse?" I tossed back.

"What if I am?"

I sighed. "What's this about? Do *you* want to fuck him?" I was trying not to think about Kieran, I wanted to be here with Brant and only Brant.

"Maybe I do." His expression was intense. "Maybe I have."

I clenched my thighs together thinking about it. He said the dirtiest things. "Then maybe you should leave me out of it."

"That's the thing, Claire. You need to be honest with yourself about what you want. And you don't want to be left out of it." He pushed his fingers through my hair and pulled me back down to his erection. "You want to be doing this right now and have Kieran taking you from behind."

"What kind of game are you playing?" Why did this have to be so complicated? This made me so hot and I did want it, but this was for the woman I pretended to be, not the woman I really was.

And it would be naïve of me not to think of the fallout. It would feel good until after, until we had to examine our emotions.

"The one where everyone wins. Strip for me," he commanded in a stern voice.

Honestly, I'd rather just give him the BJ fully clothed. "I don't—"

"I want to see you. If you don't trust me to look at you, how can you trust me to fuck you? You're beautiful. Show me." His tone was gentler now.

I'd decided I wanted to do this for him. I wanted to please him, and this was what he'd asked of me. He wanted me to strip for him.

And for some reason, I wanted to cry.

No, not some reason. A million reasons. All the sniping little comments that played in my head on repeat. I didn't want to be bare in front of him, my body exposed—all of my fat out there for him to see.

It was stupid. It wasn't like there was anything there that wasn't in the dark. I knew that. He'd seen me naked before. His dick was still hard. He still wanted me.

But I didn't want myself.

So I didn't understand how he could want me.

"You let me finger you until you came on a public boat tour, but you won't strip for me in your room where no one but me can see you?"

"I... can't." I almost choked on the words. I guess the fallout had already started. I couldn't stop thinking long enough to feel.

He pulled me to my feet, slid his hands up my thighs and up my shirt to cup my breasts and then back down to my waist where he undid the snap on my jeans.

"Take it off for me, baby." Brant tugged them down my legs and I stepped out of them.

When his hands were on me, it was different somehow. When he was taking my clothes off, it was okay. But if I had to do it, I felt like an ugly bug under a microscope. He unsnapped my bra with a quick motion.

"You're so beautiful. Won't you let me look at you?"

It might have been the pleading in his voice, I don't know. But I took off my shirt and shrugged my bra to the floor. I wanted to close my eyes so I couldn't see him looking at me.

I didn't have to acknowledge my own flesh.

He drew my hand down to his cock. "Feel what you do to me. How much I want you."

I sank to my knees again, both to taste him and to hide.

He traced his thumb over my cheek and it was somehow more intimate than all the rest of it.

Something warm surged in my chest—I didn't want to name it. It was too much, too soon.

His attention was suddenly on the door, and the shadow filling the space between the door and frame where it had drifted open.

My gaze followed his in this awful slow motion that reminded me of horror films where the audience screamed at the screen. I didn't need any sort of confirmation to know that it was Kieran. Shame burned my face and my eyes watered. I wondered what he'd seen. What he'd heard.

How long had he been standing there?

I was frozen in place, bile rising in my throat.

"Do you want him to come in?" Brant asked softly.

"Please don't toy with me." That's all this could be, some kind of fucked up bet. Something for them to laugh about later. Only, I knew Keiran wouldn't do that to me, and Brant had been so kind, so…perfect.

"Look at me."

I raised my chin to look into his eyes and I didn't need him to say anything else. I could see his sincerity, his lust.

So I nodded. God help me, I nodded.

The door creaked open wider and I couldn't look at him, couldn't face Kieran. This still wasn't real to me. Not even when another set of hands stroked down my spine and grabbed my hips.

Not even when they worked between my legs.

I focused on Brant, on taking him higher. I couldn't think about Kieran, that it was his hands touching me, pushing inside of me. That he was here, with us. But Brant wouldn't let me get away with that.

He stopped me and lifted my chin. I knew what he wanted me to do without him saying a word. He wanted me to turn, acknowledge Kieran. Touch him. Let him touch me.

He wanted to watch us.

It seemed a little twisted—not that he wanted to watch me with another man, but that it was a man I had feelings for. A man he knew I was in love with.

I turned to face Kieran, and seeing him drove this all home for me. This was actually happening.

This wasn't anything like how I'd imagined being with Kieran. There was no drunken revelry that had brought us here, no accidental touching, or unintended intimacies. There hadn't even been some friendly cuddling that had morphed into a passionate makeout session.

He was here to fuck me. Not to love me, not to solidify any bond—it was pure fucking. He didn't wait for me to peel his clothes off, he was already naked. Only I didn't know if he was Kieran or Finn McCool.

In the moment, I didn't care.

I could have him.

I swallowed hard and reached out to push that lock of hair away from his forehead. His lashes fluttered down as his eyes closed and he leaned into the caress. But it was like that shattered some wall because when his eyes opened, he jerked me against him hard and kissed me like it was my punishment rather than my reward.

He was so big everywhere. His hands, his shoulders, the sheer breadth of him. Kieran made me feel small, delicate.

He still tasted of sweet mints, but I didn't care. He wasn't with April, he was here with me. It was my body he touched, my thigh his erection was pressed against. Me. He wanted me.

Elation soared on wax wings, but I couldn't let myself think anymore. If I did, in two minutes, I'd run from the room embarrassed and ashamed. Ashamed at what I wanted, ashamed knowing they'd both seen me naked when I didn't even want to see myself naked... so much bullshit wrapped up in a ragged little ribbon.

I wanted to be done with that.

I wanted to be this version of me. The version that took people at their word, the version that thought she deserved to be treated well, that found beauty in her own body and could believe that others did too.

He picked me up easily and perched me on the bed and that's when Brant took over. I could tell that they had done this with other women before. I thought that would make me jealous, but it didn't. I liked that it wasn't awkward, or—I'd always imagined that in a threesome that choreography would be difficult. It'd be like blocking a play or shooting a porno. Not that I'd ever done a porno—obviously.

Brant shifted me to his lap into a position like reverse cowgirl, only his thighs were spread wide. I thought for a moment I'd fall, but Kieran took my hands so I could balance myself against his shoulders.

I shifted against Brant and the burn inside me flared—I rolled my hips until he was inside me. Brant's hands were on my breasts, Kieran's on my hips. He moved me, guided me, then he kissed me again.

"How many times can we make you come, Claire?" Kieran whispered against my mouth and moved his fingers to my clit, all the while, Brant was still thrusting up into me.

"Try and find out." I couldn't believe that was me. I sounded like some sex goddess. In all honesty, this all still seemed so unreal.

"I think that's a challenge," Brant said. He picked me up as easily as Kieran had and moved me until I was flat on my back and he loomed over me. Kieran pulled me close to the edge of the bed and hooked my legs over his shoulders.

"Aye, it is." His accent was thick now and I shivered. "So it does work on you, lass? Want to see what else I can do with my tongue?" He dipped his head.

The logical part of my brain assumed I was dead and this was heaven and it was the dreamer that told me this could happen to me. This was my life. I was done being a passive ghost in my own fantasy.

"Straddle me," I demanded from Brant.

He obliged, his powerful thighs caging me and I took his cock in my mouth, determined now more than ever to give him the pleasure he'd given me.

"Jesus, Claire." Brant growled low in his throat.

It was hard to concentrate with Kieran's tongue proving that he was one of the most gifted of men, but if I hadn't had Brant to focus on, I already would've dissolved into bliss. There was so much sensation, I didn't know what to feel or how to distill it down to one thing. Brant pulled away just as my climax hit me and I didn't protest, all I could do was whimper and let the waves carry me where they would.

Kieran's fingers dug into my thighs and I knew I'd have bruises the next day, and I kind of wanted them. I wanted to remember this had actually happened.

Kieran was up on the bed with us and I was pressed between them. Suddenly, it occurred to me that there were two of them and one me. That meant if we were all going to be pleasured someone would have to—I opened my mouth to speak and Kieran kissed me, silencing my protests.

His hands, Brant's hands, they moved over my skin, teasing and taunting, driving my desire that had been so recently quenched back to a frenzied pitch.

I twisted my head away from Kieran and his kiss to Brant. He kissed me too, but it was softer, sweeter. He moved to the corner of my mouth, to my cheek, then to the shell of my ear where he whispered, "Trust me."

If anyone else had said that, I would have called bullshit. But I did trust him.

"If it's uncomfortable, or you don't like it, I'll stop. I won't hurt you."

I believed him. Even when he twisted away and pulled out a small bottle of lube from my nightstand that I hadn't put there. He'd planned this, but I knew if I told him I didn't want to do this, he'd stop.

The truth was that I did want to do it.

Kieran turned me back to him and pulled my leg up high on his hip so that I was spread for them both. Brant kissed my neck, and his hand slid down over my belly and between Kieran and I to rub my clit.

We all moved together in unexpected synchronicity, writhing and seeking more friction. Kieran wasn't shy about demanding all of my attention, and whenever I'd try to turn to kiss Brant, he'd turn me back to him.

When Kieran pushed into me, I'd expected a symphony or something. But it wasn't special, there wasn't any connection. It felt good, of course, he knew what he was doing. It just wasn't…how I fantasized. Maybe that was the problem, I'd fantasized about him for too long for the reality to ever measure up.

I concentrated on the sensation, on what it was like to feel so worshipped and beautiful. Brant was ever so careful with me, teasing me and driving my arousal as high as he could before he eased against my opening. I stiffened, but Brant's voice in my ear soothed me.

"Remember, I won't hurt you. Only pleasure, sweetheart."

His fingers kept teasing me, keeping me just at the edge, but knowing somehow when I was about to careen over the ledge. He was oh-so careful and when he was inside me too, I was almost afraid to feel it. Afraid that it would go from pleasant to pain, but it didn't.

I was so full, so stretched, and I wasn't sure if I was dying or being reborn. Maybe both. I wanted it to last forever, but I wanted it to be over too. I needed to see the end of the spiral, I was falling too fast and I wanted to land somewhere good.

Kieran leaned over my shoulder. "Let her come."

We were a tangle of limbs, sweat, and bliss when I was finally launched over the edge. I was aware of nothing but starbursts and earthquakes.

I lay there, shuddering as I fell back into myself and Brant was already up and getting dressed.

"Where you going?" I mumbled, my lips numb. In fact, my whole face was numb, my fingertips and toes were tingling.

"I've still got to go to work." He kissed my cheek and looked at me for a long moment. "I'll miss you, Claire."

"I'll miss you, too." I didn't want him to go.

"Will you miss me too, Brant?" Kieran raised a brow and a self-satisfied grin spread across his face.

"No, jackass. You have to work, too. Remember?"

Kieran shrugged. "Fuck it. I'm staying right here."

"You can come back over after work," I offered.

"I'll call you." He kissed me again and got out of there like my face was on fire.

The part of me that wanted to be naïve wondered what was wrong with him, but deep down I knew. He didn't want to come back to go to bed with Kieran and I, he wanted to be with me. Kieran was supposed to be disposable and Brant entered in to this knowing that Kieran wasn't a throwaway for me.

I'd just had the time of my life, but I wasn't sure if the emotional fallout was worth it.

FAT

CHAPTER ELEVEN

Alone with Kieran, I suddenly didn't know how to act. This had been a one-off. We were still friends, but… right? I'd fucked Finn McCool, not Kieran.

Only earlier, he'd said they were one and the same.

Feeling uncomfortable and unsure, I needed a shower. Not only for emotional distance, but I was sticky *everywhere*.

I started to get up, but Kieran grabbed my hand.

"Don't run away from me now."

That's what I was doing, running. That's what I always did. It was safer.

"I just need a shower."

"I'll come with you."

"I don't think I'll get very clean."

"We'll get clean and then dirty again." Kieran pinned me on my back with one swift motion. "Or dirtier first."

I didn't have a chance to answer because my legs hooked around his waist and even though I felt rode hard and put away wet, I still arched up to meet him.

This time was different. This time, he touched my face like it was something precious to him. I couldn't help but wonder if he'd done this to April.

Fucking fuck fucker. Why couldn't I just have this moment without thinking about her? Or what Kieran had done with her? What did it matter? He was here with me now. Not her. I won. I had what I wanted.

I looked into Kieran's eyes and held his gaze through every thrust and this time, it was kind of like how I imagined it would be. How I wanted it to be.

"I love you." His voice was a jagged whisper, almost like the confession was painful for him, razorblades on his tongue. He buried his face in my neck and I knew I was making love to Kieran Holt, not fucking Finn McCool.

This was what was mine. "I love you, too. I always have."

He groaned against me, the words seeming to elicit something more in him than just the rhythmic thrusts of our lovemaking. His embrace tightened and in that moment, I had everything I ever wanted.

Except I felt like I'd betrayed Brant. His place in the bed next to us was still warm and the look on his face… when he said he'd call me, it seemed like a final goodbye.

But that didn't make any sense. He'd set this up.

The same way Kieran had pushed me to go out with Brant.

I wasn't in love with Brant. I was in love with Kieran.

So why did this feel suddenly wrong?

"Hey, come back to me," Keiran said against my ear.

"I'm here." I dug my nails into his shoulders, inhaled the familiar scent of him and focused on just how it felt to be there with him.

"Say you're mine, Claire."

"I'm yours. Always."

He shuddered against me, spent. Kieran rested his head on my breast and I held him there for a long time. I knew if I moved, it would shatter the idyll. I'd have to start thinking about all the stuff I'd put on hold to have this experience.

I'd have to think about what it meant if he loved me.

He'd said it, but I realized I didn't believe him. If he loved me, if he wanted me, why hadn't he said something?

The same reason I hadn't?

No. He's only here because he thought he was going to lose you to Brant. He doesn't want you, but he needs you.

My phone buzzed and thinking it was Brant, I stretched to reach it, but I dropped it.

"Fuck 'em. Whoever it is, they can fuck off," Kieran grumbled.

"It might be important."

"More important than what I'm about to do to you? *Again*?" He pounced on me when I squirmed away from him, but I shimmied to reach the phone on the floor and picked it up.

"Hello?"

"Claire?" It was April and I'd never heard her sound so… fragile.

"Yeah, what's up?"

"My dick," Keiran answered and tried to wrestle the phone away from me.

"Stop it. Come on. It's April." I pushed at his shoulders and he froze.

"Is he..." April began, but didn't finish her statement. Silence reigned for a moment that seemed to last forever.

I knew what she was asking and the mean girl in me was more than happy to tell her that I had what she wanted. Not because I wanted to hurt her, but because she always got everything. And for once, I got something she wanted. For once, I was good enough.

For once, it was about me.

"Yeah." There was so much in that one word. It was a knife, it was a balm, it was the culmination of all my doubts, and all of hers. I changed everything with that word.

Apparently, Kieran thought so too. His face had gone ashen.

Maybe he really did want her instead.

"I can't talk," April choked and hung up the phone.

I looked at it dumbly, the piece of technology in my hand. I glanced back and forth between the phone and Kieran.

"I didn't want to hurt her," he said.

The mean girl in me raged. Who cared? If he didn't care about hurting Brant, why should it matter how April felt? April didn't care how anyone else felt. But the woman I wanted to be, the one who I was trying so hard to become, she just nodded. "I don't want to hurt anyone."

"I shouldn't have invited her to breakfast. I should have kept everything the same. But I thought since we were friends… I knew this would happen. I warned her."

"I did too, but that doesn't change how shitty it feels, does it?" Even though those words were hollow, considering I was still doing a poisonous little cheer.

"No, it doesn't. She's the only one who ever said she wanted something other than Finn."

"That's not true."

He studied me hard, another one of those seconds that loomed into the eternal. "You never wanted Finn at all. She said she wanted both."

I decided then that words should be licensed the same as firearms because they were just as deadly.

"I'm going to grab that shower now." I fled from him, from the accusation, from the possibility that it might be true.

He didn't stop me, but a few moments later with the hot water running over my body, I heard the door creak open.

"I don't want April," he said quietly.

With the curtain between us, it was easier to speak, I felt protected. Which was dumb, it was just a stupid piece of plastic. "It's okay if you do. What happened—" I tried not to choke on the words "—it can just be something that happened. Something we tried together. It doesn't have to change us."

"We're already changed and I can't pretend we aren't. I don't want to pretend we aren't."

"Me either." I leaned back under the water, the heat comforting. "But I don't want to lose you either. I don't want you to feel…" I inhaled deeply, searching for the right words. Or maybe it was just the strength to say the right words. "I don't want you to feel like because you live here, if you don't give me what I want, that you'll lose anything."

"What do you mean?"

"You don't have to fuck me to live here. Or to still be my friend." I inhaled again, as if that would fortify me. "Or for me to love you. I'll always love you, Kieran. Always."

"I've wanted you since the moment we met."

I peeked out from behind the curtain. I had to see the expression on his face. I needed to reassure myself he was telling the truth.

"Then why didn't you say so?"

"Because I wanted to keep something in my life that wasn't tainted by my dick." He looked so haunted then it almost broke my heart.

"Why do you do the job that you do if you think your dick taints everything?" Water dripped down my cheek and he smoothed it away with the pad of his thumb.

"Because it's what I'm good at."

"You're good at a lot of things. The way you suped up your car with your own hands? Not everyone can do that."

"Bollocks. That's a simple thing, lass."

"For you. Not for everyone." I ducked back behind the curtain and finished washing my hair.

"I didn't mean for this to happen," he said after a while. "With Brant I mean. I really thought you'd be good together."

"We are," I admitted. "But I've always been in love with you."

"Part of me wonders if it's fair that we have to hurt all our friends to be together."

I swallowed hard, dreading what he would say next. That it was all over. This was a fluke. We shouldn't have done it.

"But then I realize fuck them. It's not our fault if we're in love. It happened. They can either be happy for us or fuck off."

Could it be that simple? Did I want it to be? Was I ready to give up all of my friendships just to be with Kieran? A few weeks ago, I would have said yes.

Who was I kidding? Of course I'd say yes. I'd wanted him for so long and now he was mine. I wasn't going to throw away everything I'd ever wanted with both hands. I didn't want to hurt Brant, I didn't want to hurt April, but it was okay for me to be happy, right? I'd lived a long time worrying about making other people happy, worrying about what other people thought. It was time for me.

"Right. They can all fuck off. We have each other."

"That's my girl." He pulled the curtain back and I squealed, but he tugged me against him anyway and kissed me hard.

His kiss convinced me everything would be okay.

"Oh my god, I'm so sore. I can't do this again," I giggled. It was a good sore though, it was something I could get used to.

"That's good lass, because I don't think I can do it again. At least not for another hour." He grinned.

I clenched my thighs, thinking of it. If he wanted me again even if it hurt, I'd let him. "Actually, I need to go to the store."

"What? Why? We don't have anywhere we have to be. I just want to stay in your bed. Until tomorrow. Then we can stay in my bed."

I laughed. "We had sex without a condom."

"Aren't you on something?" he questioned.

"No."

His eyes widened. "Why the fuck not?"

"It makes me sick."

"Oh Jaysus."

"No, it's fine. Don't lose your shit. I'll just get the morning after pill. It'll be fine." The water was starting to get cold.

"It needs to be."

His response pissed me off at first, but he looked so terrified, that I couldn't stay angry. I mean, he could have gotten a condom. Brant never—I couldn't start down that road. "Kieran," I said his name to make him look at me, really look at me. "It will be. I promise."

"I guess we need to talk."

"I thought that was what we were doing?" I turned off the water. "Hand me a towel."

I wrapped the towel around my body and one around my hair before stepping out on to the bathmat.

"There's more I need to tell you. You may not want to be with me after."

"Unless you kick puppies for fun, or you're a serial killer, there's nothing you can tell me that's going to change my mind." I realized that he needed as much reassurance as I did.

"Even if I said that I don't want children? Not just not now, not ever."

I considered. "I guess we should've had this talk before we started having sex." I gave a self-deprecating laugh. "I can't say what I'll want in the future, but right now, I don't either. Now, I know that comes with being with you. I accept that."

"Can you really?"

"Not all women want children. I wouldn't want to just have them to have them. I'm in love with you, and that means all of you."

"Even Finn?"

I bit my lip. "I guess even Finn."

"You guess?" He raised a black brow. We were back in playful territory. Back where we were both comfortable.

"Well, you know, Kieran is better in bed than Finn."

"When did you ever sleep with Finn?"

"Finn and Brant. After Brant left, then you were Kieran."

"You do know me."

"Was that in doubt?"

"I guess not." He grinned. "So where do we have to go to get this thing?"

"Just to the pharmacy. I can go myself. It's no big deal." Except I really did want him to go with me. I was an adult, I could handle my reproductive choices alone if I had to, but I really wanted him to do it with me for some reason.

Maybe because I was still kind of irritated about the condom. I could have spoken up, I should have told them to wear them. That was on me, too. I couldn't think about how many women either of them had been with or it would turn my stomach.

Which was completely hypocritical of me, but I couldn't help how it made me feel. Although I could help how I reacted to it.

"I'll go with you. Then we can get dinner."

"Okay, let me get dressed."

I thought about the takeout Brant had brought me sitting in its styrofoam container. I picked it up when I walked into the room and carried it out to the fridge.

He wasn't going to call me.

He wasn't coming back.

When he said he'd miss me, it wasn't just tonight. That certainty clanged through my head like a bell.

There was a pang deep under my ribs that I couldn't explain, so I didn't think about it. Instead, I got dressed.

On the ride to the pharmacy, I enjoyed my newfound freedom to touch Kieran as I chose, to indulge my every urge to be close to him and it was an amazing feeling. I kissed down his neck, nipped at his ear, ran my hands over his thighs.

Who would've thought I'd have ended up here?

God, I loved him so much it hurt. If I'd thought being with Kieran was like a razorblade when I didn't speak of it, it was sharper somehow now that I could. I was so afraid I'd wake up and this would all be a dream. I'd fallen asleep petting his hair last Saturday and I hadn't woken up.

I inhaled the scent of him and he still smelled like sex—he smelled like us. It was like I'd marked him with it. I liked that.

He followed me in to the pharmacy after we'd parked and I headed straight back to the prescription counter. I'd never done this for myself before, but I'd brought April a few times.

"Plan B, please."

The pharmacy tech looked at me for a moment. "ID please?"

I handed her my ID and she looked at the ID and at me. "Is everything on here correct?"

They'd never asked April that. I might have lied about my weight.

My guts roiled and twisted. "My weight has changed."

She leaned toward me, at least making an attempt to be discreet. "Plan B might not be an effective option for you. It's found to be unreliable for women over one-hundred and seventy-five pounds. I won't tell you not to buy it, but if you're worried you might be pregnant, watch your cycle closely."

I turned to look at Kieran who obviously hadn't heard her. He was tapping his foot to the elevator music and looking around the store like a kid waiting for his mom to be done shopping.

I nodded, but I said, "Thanks. I'll take it anyway."

She rang it up and I swiped my debit card.

Loaded up with the neatly stapled bag, I wondered if I should tell Kieran what the tech had told me. Then I thought about his earlier reaction. There was no reason to drive it into the ground.

It would give him peace of mind. If I ended up pregnant, well, I'd deal with it. I couldn't even think about that now.

A small, nagging voice in the back of my head said that I could've told Brant about it. In fact, I wouldn't have thought twice about telling him.

They were different men, I had to stop comparing them.

When we were out in the car, I said, "Let's grab a pizza. I don't want to take this on an empty stomach."

"You got it, baby."

It occurred to me that he didn't bother to buy any condoms.

FAT

CHAPTER TWELVE

It was both familiar and strange waking up in bed with Kieran.

I still wondered if I was dreaming.

But the pounding on the door that slammed through my head didn't seem to be a dream at all.

"Fucking hell, someone better be dead." Kieran rolled over and dragged me beneath the covers with him. I'd have been content to curl in his arms and go back to sleep if only the pounding would stop.

He growled and slid out of bed.

He was naked.

"Are you going to get dressed?"

"No. They deserve the wrath of my manhood if they can't wait until a decent hour."

I looked at the clock on the table. It was noon. I couldn't believe I'd slept so long. I started to get up.

"Lass, if you budge just one centimeter off that bed, whoever is at the door is going to die a slow death. I have plans for you today." He winked at me.

I got off the bed anyway. I wanted to see who was at the door.

Kieran opened the door, giving me a view of his gorgeous, tight ass and our visitor, whoever they were, a view of his…

I recognized her voice. She'd been one of many of the pussy parade as I'd come to call it.

The nasty voice in my head said I could now join their club.

It was cordially invited to shut up. This was my house, and my Kieran.

"I just wanted to make sure you were okay," she said. "You weren't at the club last night and you promised you'd be there for my bachelorette party."

I was torn between telling him to make good on his promise somehow because it was bad for business if he didn't. I couldn't let him screw up at work just because we were together. He said this was what he loved doing and I wouldn't screw up *Chubbalicious* for him—or anyone for that matter.

But me in girlfriend mode wanted to rip that girl's eyes out of her head and stomp them into Jell-O. I reminded myself that this was part of dating Kieran. This would have been part of dating Brant, too.

"Something came up."

She gave him a once over, looking him up and down. "I can see that it did." I heard her giggle. "And it's still up."

Kieran laughed and the sound grated on my nerves.

"Do you need some help with that?"

"I thought I was supposed to dance for your bachelorette party?"

"You were."

"How does your husband-to-be feel about your fucking other men?" Kieran asked in a soft voice.

"The same way I feel about him fucking his secretary."

"Are you sure you should be marrying him?"

"I'm sure I should still be fucking you."

"I'm seeing someone."

The woman laughed. "So who is the paragon of femininity that finally caught you, Finn? She must be a supermodel."

I looked down at myself. *Hardly.* I waited with baited breath to see what he'd say, what he'd do. I think I half expected him to go outside and bang her in his car and come back inside like nothing had ever happened. Or he'd tell her to wait for him because he'd had a brain tumor for dinner and hooked up with his homely roommate…

"Most beautiful woman in the world."

I snorted and almost choked on my own spit, but it sounded like he meant it.

"If things don't work out, you have my number."

I debated jumping back into the bed, but I didn't want to hide that I'd been listening. Hiding things was never a good way to start a relationship.

When he came back to the bedroom, he said, "What did I say, woman?"

I laughed. "Most beautiful woman in the world, huh?"

"Aye."

"What have I told you about getting cute?"

"And what've I told you? I'm already cute." He winked and snatched me up in his arms as if I weighed nothing.

I curled my arm around his neck. "I could get used to this."

"I'll carry you around all day if you want."

"Yes, that's what we'll do. When *Chubbalicious* is a success, you'll be my cabana boy/bodyguard."

"If that's what you want."

Everything I felt with him was a double-edged sword. Initially, the idea of him being all mine all the time thrilled me. But then I wondered what he wanted out of life, what he was passionate about. He had to be passionate about something besides putting his dick in me. Not that the idea wasn't great for my self-esteem, but he was a person, a whole entity who existed outside of our relationship matrix.

Jesus. Why did I have to pick everything apart? Why couldn't I just be happy?

"What about you? What do you want?" I asked him.

"To spend the day in bed with you."

He was being purposefully obtuse. "As lovely as that sounds, I do have to work today."

"No, you don't. Not unless you're working me."

"I still have a few things to get done before the launch."

"I guess I'll just have to persuade you." He laughed. "I need you this morning. At least twice."

"You're kind of a high-maintenance boyfriend," I teased, but allowed him to carry me to the bathroom.

"You have no idea, but we'll compromise this morning."

He wasn't kidding.

After a leisurely shower and two bouts of sex, I was fairly certain I wasn't going to be able to sit comfortably for a week. Everything hurt, but it was a good kind of hurt. The kind that with every step I took, every twinge of discomfort, I remembered what I'd done to put myself in that kind of state.

As I made us breakfast, I kept sneaking glances at him out of the corner of my eye, once again wondering how I'd gotten this lucky.

"If you keep looking at me like that, I'll have you flat on your back again in about five seconds."

"Oh my god, how can you go again? I really might die."

He laughed. "I'm addicted to you, what can I say?"

I blushed and plated our food.

For such a big guy, he moved quickly. His hands were on my hips and he nuzzled my neck. "How did I get so lucky?"

For the first time, I'd gotten something I wanted. I'd had to give up some things to have it, but it was mine. Kieran was all I needed.

I didn't flinch when he ran his hands down over my belly, he'd seen me naked a lot and he still wanted to touch me, still wanted to be with me. Maybe this was real. Maybe all the stuff I'd been telling myself was true and it was the little voice inside my head that was the damn dirty liar.

"Since you're working today, I thought I'd go in to work tonight to make up for last night." He watched me like he thought I was a ticking bomb.

What was I going to say? I knew what he did for a living. So I smiled. "I'm glad you stayed with me yesterday. I don't know that we'd be at this point—together—if you hadn't. But I get it. You have to work. We both have to live in the real world, too."

The tension leached out of him. "Thank Jaysus." He kissed the top of my head. "I'm glad the girlfriend hat didn't turn you into some needy freak."

"Did you think it would?" I guess that still remained to be seen. I don't know why it was okay in my head for Brant to still work there when he was seeing me, but Kieran… It twisted me up.

That stupid voice was back—God, I was such a fucking psycho. But that voice said that it was because Kieran couldn't be trusted. A man didn't simply stop fucking a new woman every night. It takes thirty days to form a habit or break one and he'd been doing this for years.

"I think we should establish some boundaries if this is going to work. What's okay, what's not."

I'd have rather just stuck my head in the sand, but he was right. This was my chance to tell him what I wanted, what would hurt me and what I didn't care about. Then I couldn't claim the injured party if we'd hashed it all out, and neither could he.

Communication. That's what relationships were really about. The attraction and sex were all great, but it would all fall apart without talking about expectations—both reasonable and unreasonable. I knew that.

I had this nervous habit of biting my lip, but my mouth was so raw from our sessions, I stopped myself in time.

"I don't want you to come to the club anymore," he blurted.

My first instinct was to think that it was because he wanted to hide something from me. "Why?"

"Because I've seen the guys who let their girlfriends come to the club."

"I didn't freak out on Brant."

"Yeah, but you weren't in love with him, right?"

I processed that. I wasn't in love with Brant, but I'd thought of him as mine, after a fashion.

"Right?" he asked again.

"Right." I nodded. "But I know it's your job. I have to say, it makes me uncomfortable to be told you don't want me to go."

"Don't you trust me?"

"I think that goes both ways. I have to trust you're not going to cheat on me and you have to trust that I understand what your job entails. If I can't watch you work, we shouldn't be in a relationship."

"I know that." His voice was quiet.

"Then, what—" I braced my hands on the counter. "I see. You don't think this is going to work."

"I want it to."

"It can't if we don't trust each other."

"I certainly don't want to see you with your hands all over some other man. I know it's backwards as fuck that I expect you to tolerate it, but I just can't."

That shouldn't have pleased me, but I did. I should have called him on the double-standard, but it didn't bother me.

"Okay."

"Really? Just... okay?"

I shrugged. "Why not? It's not a big deal to me. I don't need to punish you because of your job or hold my breath for something that's not important to me just to prove a point."

"So what is important to you?"

"That you come home after work. I don't want to be staring at the clock at five in the morning wondering where you're at or who you're with. If you change your mind about being with me, that you tell me."

"I can do that. What else? I know there's something that you're holding back."

There was, but I looked away from him. "I don't want you to take any more hotel calls. I know they're more than private dances, strip-o-grams or whatever you want to call them. And I know it'll eat into your money, but I also know you fuck most of them."

I'd just said to myself that I wouldn't ruin Chubbalicious for him, that I didn't expect him to give up his work for me, but that was a hard limit. I guessed it was my turn to have a double-standard.

"Claire, it was really hard to set that up. If I ever need that income back…"

"Are you telling me no?" I asked quietly.

He shook his head. "I'm asking you to wait until you make sure I'm what you really want, that we're forever."

"So it's supposed to be okay for you to fuck other people?"

"Finn, not me."

I nodded slowly. "But you told me the other day that Finn was you. You can't have it both ways. Make up your mind."

"They don't mean anything but a zero on a check."

"Then why would it be so hard for you to just stop?"

He didn't have an answer for me.

"That's a hard limit, Kieran."

"Are you kidding me?"

I could ask him the same. "Really? What about if I put an ad in the paper and started taking money for "erotic massage" or "dancing"? Would that be okay?"

"No," he growled.

"Why?"

He didn't answer me.

"Why, Kieran?" I'd raised my voice. "Answer me."

"They wouldn't hire you anyway."

I don't know if he'd meant to kill me, but he did. There was something in me that withered and died when he said that, but I refused to break in front of him. Instead, I lifted my chin and stared at him until he could meet my eyes.

"I didn't mean that," he said.

"You don't have to apologize for speaking the truth. You're right. A traditional service wouldn't hire me, but there are plenty of men who like thick women. Maybe I'll start my own service right out of the house. Yeah, I think I will."

"Claire, I just… Christ." He pushed his fingers through his hair and the look on his face mirrored what I felt inside. "I shouldn't have—I was defending myself."

"Against what?"

"Against the truth. No, you can't go sell yourself. You don't have to. You can do so many other things. I can't. This is all I have, all I'm good at."

"Fucking spare me the sob story. That's a cop out. It's a sad little boy who wants everything to be done for him and when it gets hard, he just gives up and goes back to what's easiest."

"What's wrong with easy?" He completely missed my point.

"Nothing is wrong with easy, but you keep acting like you have no choice. Like the life you live isn't wholly and solely up to you and it is."

"This is why I don't date."

"Really? You're going to go there?" I shook my head. "Dancing is your job. Fucking is a choice."

"That pays well. What does it matter if it's Finn and not me?"

"Where shall I start? The part where you stick your dick in people you don't know and then you want to fuck me without a condom?" Dear God, I had to get tested. I swallowed hard. "Or the part where you being with another woman hurts me. It doesn't matter if it's Finn or Kieran. It's still you."

"Give up *Chubbalicious*, then."

"Why?"

"It's the same thing."

"No, it's really not."

"Because dancing and pleasure aren't viable careers, right?" he snapped.

"That's not what I said. I didn't ask you to stop dancing. That's not illegal. Whoring yourself is."

"So now I'm a whore?"

"You said so yourself." I wasn't backing down from this, even though I knew what that meant. As soon as I'd gotten Kieran, I'd lost him, but I wasn't going to make it easy for him. I wasn't going to say I was done so he could go cry to himself about how horrible women were and about how no one understood him. I understood him better than he understood himself.

"I don't want to fight with you and I'm not trying to hurt you. But that's where I stand. Why don't we both think about where we're going and where we want to be and talk about it later?"

"I've got a call tonight and I'm taking it."

My nose prickled like I'd been punched and I knew I was about to cry. "Be sure that's what you want to do."

I went to my room and closed the door. I had to fight not to slam it, but instead, I gently clicked the lock into place with shaking hands. I melted into my quilt without letting the tears fall.

CHAPTER THIRTEEN

I didn't come out of my room for the rest of the day. I tried to work on *Chubbalicious*, but my heart wasn't in it.

I got an email from Ryan, the photographer, with all of the images attached. Hollie and Rosa looked great. I didn't even want to look at mine and I shouldn't have.

Everyone said I looked so good at the shoot, that I was so hot, but all I could see was my double chin. Or my ass looked too wide, my thighs to fat, and the rolls around my middle were disgusting. I hated the sight of myself and I kind of wanted to gouge everyone's eyes out who'd ever seen this picture or who ever would.

This was in Ryan's portfolio. He was going to show that to people.

They wouldn't hire you.

No, they wouldn't hire me to sleep with anyone.

I slammed the lid on my laptop closed.

Kieran didn't love me. He was with me because he thought my self-esteem was bad enough that I'd put up with whatever he wanted to do and I'd never leave him. I wasn't a threat to his fear of abandonment because he didn't think I could get anyone else.

This thing with Brant, he just wanted to prove I still belonged to him.

In that moment, for all that I loved Kieran, I kind of hated him, too.

I'd read all the self-help books about loving myself, about not allowing myself to feel inferior, that I had to give permission to let other people's comments and actions elicit any reaction from me.

But I wasn't ice or stone. I was just a fat girl trying to fake until she made it.

My phone rang and when I saw it was April, I swiped to reject the call. She called back and I rejected it again and turned my phone off. I just couldn't deal with her shit. I had my own to worry about. I get that she was hurt by what happened with Kieran, but she knew what she was getting into.

I guess I should have too.

I didn't know how long I lay there staring at the ceiling, waiting for the numbness to give way to something else. It never did.

Not even when another loud banging commenced on the door. I ignored it until a short time later, there was a tap on my window. Someone was really determined.

"Fuck off."

"It's me," Brant said.

I went to the window and opened the blinds, then pushed up the glass. I saw it was creeping on dawn. Purple and orange tendrils streaked the sky. I'd lay there in my own misery and stewed all night. How pathetic was that?

And Kieran hadn't come home.

It was the mother of all battles to keep my expression neutral as the realization washed over me.

"What's up?"

"Can you let us in? Kieran lost his keys."

I raised a brow. Part of me wanted to say fuck him. He could come home when he dug them out of whatever skank he'd left them in, but I didn't get to be angry. He'd been honest with me.

"Why isn't Kieran tap-tapping on my window?"

Brant looked as if he was ashamed for Kieran. "God, Claire. I didn't even want to bring him home. I told him to crash on my couch, but he…" Brant just kept shaking his head.

"How drunk is he?"

"You're not going to let him in?"

I sighed and pulled my robe more tightly around my waist. "I'll be there in a second." I closed the window.

Brant and Austin dragged him inside, and he stumbled. He wasn't quite ready to pass out, but he was close.

"You mad, baby?" he slurred.

"You guys know where his room is." I turned to go back to my own room.

"What's going on?" Brant asked.

"I can't." I shrugged. "Just no."

"I didn't go," Kieran mumbled. "I didn't go." Brant and Austin hauled him into his room and got him settled.

I wanted to go back to my room and stew some more, but that wasn't going to help anything.

"Thanks for bringing him home."

Austin looked back and forth between me and Brant and said, "Yeah, anytime. I'm just going to wait outside."

Brant nodded and waited until the door closed behind him before he said anything. "What did you fight about?"

"I'm not doing this with you."

"Why not?" He seemed so sincere.

"You said you'd call." As if I had any right to be mad about anything.

"Oh, Claire. We both know that you and I are done. I knew that when we invited Kieran to join. Remember? I told you this was coming. I didn't need to call you after to have you tell me that you and Kieran were together."

"But we're not. Not really."

"I gathered. He was a fucking wreck tonight. He didn't dance."

"What did he do?"

Brant looked uncomfortable.

"Never mind."

"I'm not going to carry tales because I don't know what happened. April came to see him."

If any more sharp things stabbed my heart, all I'd have left in my chest was applesauce. A ton of questions bloomed rancid on my tongue, but I didn't say any of them. I wasn't going to grill Brant and put him in the middle of it.

He stuffed his hands in his pockets. "Did you get the pictures back yet from the shoot?"

I nodded. "Yeah. Hollie's and Rosa's are just what I wanted."

"What about yours?"

"We shall never speak of them again." I managed a weak smile.

"I'd like one. One of you and me?"

"I'll just forward the email, if you promise not to put it on Facebook."

"No, it's just for me."

I nodded. We stood there in awkward silence for almost a full minute.

"I should go."

"Take care of yourself."

"When I said I'd miss you, I meant it." He kissed my cheek and his lips were warm, his scent safe.

"I know. I miss you, too."

"You've got my number."

"Yeah, see, if a guy says he's going to call and doesn't, that's not usually a cue to me that I should text."

"I was giving you time. I still am."

"Time for what?"

"To be with Kieran without feeling guilty. Without worrying about hurting me or how you're going to break it off. I took care of that."

"How did you know I would? Why do you and Kieran both think you get to choose how I feel about anything?"

Brant sighed. "Do you think I would choose for you to be with him? I sure as shit didn't choose that. But when I left, if I'd said, that was a good time, but if you want to be my girl, Kieran has to go back to his own room, what would have happened there?"

I bit my lip.

"I don't want to be your second choice, Claire. I deserve better than that and so do you."

He was wrong. I didn't deserve better, but maybe he did.

"Then why did you set all this up?"

"Because I want you to be happy."

It seemed like such an easy thing—happiness. Something made of light and bubbles, but it wasn't. It was complicated and heavy, like a brick.

"I want you to be happy too." I did. I didn't want to hurt him, but if I was being honest with myself, I didn't want to give him up either.

For all that I wanted it to be about me, it couldn't just be about me.

"I know." His voice was strained.

"Then why does this hurt?" I blurted. I should have kept it to myself, let it fester with everything else.

"Because I'm something different than Kieran. Because you're looking at what he did tonight and you're thinking I'd never do that to you. And you're right, I wouldn't, but I'm not the one you're in love with. He is."

I looked back at his closed bedroom door. "I don't know what I'm feeling."

"I do. You're feeling lost and betrayed."

My gaze wandered down to my hands. "You're right. I feel so betrayed and I don't even know what happened."

"Do you trust Kieran to tell you the truth about what happened?"

"I don't know."

"That's important." He closed his eyes and sighed. "I keep waiting for you to ask me what I saw, but I don't think you're going to. I'm glad."

"I wouldn't put you in that position."

He nodded. "Take care of you, okay?"

"Yeah." I nodded. "You too."

I watched him leave and I wondered if maybe I'd screwed up. Well, I knew I'd screwed things up, I just wasn't sure what the fallout would be yet. I never should've crossed the line with Kieran. He was something better left as an unrequited fantasy. Then we'd still be friends. All of us would still be friends.

Only, I didn't miss April.

I didn't want to be her friend.

It was nice not having her voice in concert with the voice in my head taking little digs at me all the time.

But I still wanted to be Kieran's friend. I wanted to have that part of him no one else did and I was pretty sure I'd lost it.

Or worse, maybe it had just lost its luster. He wasn't some sex god to me anymore, neither was he that guy just needing the right woman, that guy who could be fixed. The one I'd warned April that he wasn't in the beginning.

He was Kieran, the keeper of my heart and he'd twisted it and torn it in half.

The sound of retching echoed from his bathroom and I looked up at the ceiling, half hoping there'd be some kind of cheat sheet with all the answers taped up to the crown molding.

I could leave him there—I should.

But I wouldn't.

"Pussy," I muttered to myself.

I braved opening his door and creeping into the bathroom. It stank of rye whiskey and stale smoke, and aftershave. He was on the floor with his head leaned back against the mint green tile on the wall. It was ugly as shit—the wall, not him—even drunk and acting the wrung out bastard, he was still beautiful as sin.

I ran a washcloth under the cool water from the tap and crouched down next to him to sponge his heated forehead.

I was thoroughly disgusted with myself. This was condoning his behavior. It was setting the standard for how he'd treat me. He'd done God knew what with God knew who and I wasn't screaming, crying, or throwing things. I wasn't even ignoring him. I was coddling him, petting him and offering him comfort.

I agreed with my earlier assessment of myself: pussy.

His hand closed over mine. "It's too much," he mumbled.

"What is?" I eased his hand back down into his lap and continued to administer to him.

"This. You. I wanted to prove to myself and to you that you'd leave."

"Why?"

He opened his eyes, dark and turbulent—gorgeous in his suffering. "Because anyone I love leaves. I fuck it up."

I cupped his cheek. "So, you fucked it up on purpose?"

He turned his head away from me, looked at everything but me.

"I see." I stood, wet the cloth some more and then drew it to the back of his neck and up on his forehead again.

"I wanted to prove to myself that I could survive it."

"I was with you until that part, slugger." My voice was a whisper. "You can survive anything."

His fingers circled my wrist. "Not losing you. I can't." His exhale deflated him. "I don't want to."

"So what did you do, Kieran?"

He didn't speak.

"You told me you were going to take that client. If all you did was what you said you were going to do, I can't fault you for that."

He cut a sharp glance in my direction.

"I didn't say I could live with the arrangement and be with you, but I won't fault you for your honesty."

"It wasn't her."

"But you did sleep with someone else." Each word was a bullet. "I don't need you to tell me anymore."

"Please."

"Please what? Please take your confession like I'm your priest? Please forgive you? Please what?" I hissed and dropped the cloth.

"Take my confession. Absolve me of my sins. Forgive me."

"Your sins are your own and I don't want to hear it. You can wear that weight alone. I don't want to know. In fact, I need not to. I don't want to see a picture of her, I don't want to imagine what it was like—the two of you together. What you were thinking about her, if you thought about me, if I matter to you. If I'm as pretty as she is. If she's skinny and if that's why you wanted to fuck her instead of me. No, I don't want it."

Even though I already knew that it was April he'd been with. If he didn't speak it aloud, I could pretend it wasn't true. It was still all circumstantial until it spewed out of his mouth like that gallon of rye he'd drank and the stench would hang in the air just the same.

I hated her in that moment. I hated her so much I could taste it like the coppery tang of blood on my tongue.

"I don't want it either and it's rotten, Claire. Rotten and sour."

"Whatever you did isn't something that happened to you. It's something that you did all on your own. You did it, you chose to do it. No one had a gun to your head."

"You did."

I snorted. "What are you talking about?

"Losing you. It was the gun to my head and I just pulled the trigger."

"You're so full of shit you can't even smell it anymore." I fled back to my room and if I was smelling my own bullshit, I'd admit that I wanted him to chase me.

I wanted him to say that he was sorry, it had all been a lie, some kind of test—and I guessed it was a test.

April would say he just needed to be saved. He needed to be loved no matter what.

I did love him. I wouldn't stop loving him.

But could I live with him banging other women every time he felt the least bit insecure so he could test me?

No. I couldn't.

The distance that had started as a small fracture had been like the dancing of tectonic plates. There wasn't just a small creek between us now, it was a glacial gorge. There'd be no shoving us back together.

I shook my head at the train of my thoughts. That was overdramatic and theatrical. Adults weren't supposed to behave that way, but I wasn't feeling much like an adult. This growing up business was bullshit.

I never thought I would miss being a kid. I couldn't wait to grow up because when I grew up, I was going to do "*all the things*." At least, that's what I told myself while I was watching cartoons. I was going to be beautiful and rich, I was going to have a great job, and I was never, ever going to treat my kids the way my mother treated me.

I was going to have babies and I was going to love them so much that they couldn't help but know they were amazing. And I'd never make them write down what they ate on a piece of paper, I'd never judge them for what they put in their mouths or how much.

A memory of a forgotten Sunday dinner washed over me—all the long hours in the kitchen with my mother. All the delicious things laid out to tease and tantalize, and I could have none of it.

It was all for some new man she'd met and she was afraid that he wouldn't want her if he knew she had a fat daughter. I wasn't allowed to eat for two days, fasting, she'd said. As if three days of only drinking water would make up for eating only macaroni breakfast, lunch and dinner for weeks on end so she could afford to have cigarettes, pedicures and get her hair done.

And as if having a fat daughter was worse than being one of those women who couldn't define herself without a man.

I remembered the way my mother always smelled of that Dollar Store perfume and in that moment, I almost missed her.

Because it would be her voice in my head telling me if I could just lose some weight, life would be so much better. It was easier to hear it in her voice than my own.

Her voice I could ignore.

But I supposed it really was her voice—it had taken up residence in my body like a parasite, suckling all the joy out of everything like marrow from my bones. The worst part was that I'd let it and I didn't know how to make it stop.

CHAPTER FOURTEEN

I couldn't avoid April forever, even though I wanted to. I didn't understand why she couldn't just leave it alone. I was done.

It wasn't just the night previous that had made that decision for me, I think it was a long time coming and when I realized that her voice was so much like my mother's, I knew it was time to cut her loose. I'd already had that in my life once before and it hadn't done anything for me.

She called several more times until she finally texted to say that she was coming over.

It was tempting to hide in my bedroom and rot.

She didn't have a key and I doubted that Kieran would be letting her in any time soon.

The very idea of her being in my house made me sick. Maybe Kieran and I weren't together, but as selfish as it was, I couldn't have it: Her. Him. In my house. Together.

Again.

I was sure that the gentle tap on my window was her.

If she tapped it again, I'd answer it. But if she was content to let it go with one tap, so was I. It would be a relief to let the friendship die quietly, rather than with an explosion.

The bitch tapped again.

Damn her.

I opened the window. "I would have thought the whole not answering your calls or texts might have been a pretty good indicator that I don't want to talk to you."

"I have some things I need to say to you."

Her face was puffy from crying. She looked bad and rather than having any empathy for her like I should have, all I could feel was a certain sense of grim satisfaction. "Because it's all about what you need to do, right?"

"Claire—"

"No. Fuck you, April. We're done."

"Over a guy? Are you kidding me?"

"I could say the same to you. I'm sorry you got your feelings hurt. But fucking Kieran now, after you knew we were together? Yeah, whatever."

She looked like I'd slapped her. "He *told* you?"

"Of course he told me. He tells me everything. He always has."

"I bet he didn't mention the part where he couldn't keep it up because all he could do was say your name and snivel in his whiskey."

"Well, look at that." I cocked my head to the side. "I guess you were wrong."

"About what?"

"About it always being about who was thinner? I guess it's not."

"Yeah, and I guess you're having a grand old time saying 'I told you so'."

"Of course I am. You would too if you were me."

"I'd never let myself be you." Her lip curled in disgust.

"Let yourself? You couldn't hack it in my skin, sweetheart." I nodded. "So whatever you think you have to say, I don't want to hear it because I don't care. So go back to your tower on high and fuck yourself while you're at it."

"Maybe I'm here to see Kieran too."

"And maybe you can take him with you because you won't be seeing him in my house."

"He can have guests."

"Not you." Christ, I knew it was petty, but at the moment, the one thing I could control was access to my own property.

"That's pathetic."

"You can paint it up in any whore's makeup you like, but after it all washes off, the answer is still the same."

"What do you think he would have to say about it?"

"That's what you keep missing, April. He doesn't get to say anything about it."

"It's sad you'd use the roof over his head to keep him."

I wasn't trying to keep him at all. I wasn't forcing him to do anything. "What's sad is that you still think I care about your opinion. Why don't you go think about why it was he couldn't keep his dick hard for you? You know that old adage it's not you, it's me? Well, it's not. It really is you."

I slammed the window closed and the blinds fell back into place.

It was a strange brew of emotion left for me. I was heartsick, but there was a manic kind of joy too.

Until Kieran opened the door to my room.

"Are you okay?" he asked.

At first, I thought that was a stupid question, but since I'd decided to lie about the answer, I guess it wasn't after all. "I'm fine."

"I heard you yelling." He peered around the room, as if someone was going to pop out from under the bed.

"That would have been April telling me how sad and pathetic I am." I nodded slowly.

He looked like refried shit. The bags under his eyes, the exhaustion written on his face, and deep pools of sadness in his eyes.

In that second, I wanted to forgive him anything and everything. I couldn't stand to see him looking so broken and lost.

"I'm sorry," he said, eyes closed, as if he couldn't stand to look at me.

"Me too." I nodded.

"What did you do?"

"I threw away our friendship."

"Are we so broken we can't be fixed?"

I studied him again and this time, he met my regard. This wasn't the same man who'd told me on the night of April's birthday how I deserved to be happy, how I should give Brant a chance... That was the Kieran I was in love with. This guy was someone different. He wasn't the Kieran I knew and he wasn't Finn McCool either.

"Why can't we just say April was my Brant and start over?"

Again, there was part of me that surrendered to this idea. That it would be okay if I could just forget about it—this was the happily ever after I wanted and the only thing standing in the way was the evil stepsister who tricked the prince.

But no one tricked him into anything.

"If you'll remember, I wasn't your girlfriend when I slept with Brant. In fact, you set us up."

"It cut me just the same."

"So every time you're hurt, this is what I can expect from you?"

"April told me that you were the reason I could never have a relationship because I was already in one with you."

"What does that even mean?" I cried.

"It means that none of the women I've been with in the last five years have mattered a damn to me except you."

It disgusted me that his statement made me feel special. It shouldn't have. It wasn't a compliment. "So April's the great sage now? Fine. You know what else she said? At the beginning of any relationship, things are the best they're ever going to be. So if this is the best it can be, it's not worth it for either of us."

"Claire—"

"No. Look, I love you. That's never been in doubt." It felt good to say it. "But you didn't trust me not to hurt you and now I don't trust you not to hurt me." I straightened and lifted my chin. I felt lighter for saying it, like I'd laid down a burden. "I did once, even though that voice in my head told me not to. You know, the one that makes me think I'll never have anything, ever be anyone. Ever be beautiful enough, smart enough… loved enough? Do you know what it's like when that voice is right?"

"I do." He nodded solemnly. "I never wanted to be that to you."

"I don't know that you do. You never net let anyone close enough to let the voice be right."

"You."

That answer was like ignition on a rocket. "Me? When, Kieran? When did I make the voice right?"

"By not forgiving me."

"This was a test and you know what, that's not how love works. Life tests us enough without testing each other. I'm supposed to feel bad that I can't be okay with you sleeping with other women? With a woman who used to be my friend?" I shook my head. "No, I'm done."

"I can't just be friends with you."

Panic threatened to strangle me, but logic overrode fear. He was manipulating me, just like the test. And April had been right on at least that, the part about how things would never be any better.

I could suddenly see why Kieran couldn't maintain a relationship with anyone. Anytime someone had expectations of him, he couldn't stand it.

Finally, I realized maybe I could be the woman I wanted to be, maybe I was actually on my way to becoming her because the way I perceived myself—that woman—she would have taken this shit because she thought she deserved it.

Or she couldn't do any better.

But I didn't deserve it.

And I could do better.

Even though my heart was breaking, I think it was a lot like re-breaking a bone to set it correctly.

"Then I guess you should look for somewhere else to live."

"You're evicting me?"

"Of course not, but if you don't even want to be my friend, we shouldn't be living in the same house."

"What are you going to do if *Chubbalicious* fails? All your money is tied up in that and this house."

"If you're not my friend, why do you care?"

"Damn it, Claire." He pushed his hand through his hair. "Things can't end like this."

"You're the one ending them. I'm trying to be your friend."

"But we're not friends, not anymore."

"Why? If we can't be friends, we sure as hell can't be lovers."

"I guess you're right. I'll start looking for a place."

It was stupid that part of me still wanted him to fight for me, for us. But I'd told him no, what did I expect?

The short answer was not this, but the long answer was much more complicated and made of fairy dust and bubbles.

"I thought you promised you'd always love me." He walked out of the room.

I always would love him, but even if I told him that, he wouldn't believe me. And it was kicking the issue to death because if I tried to reassure him, he'd think it was a door.

I'd thought that reaching for what I wanted would ruin everything and it had, just not in the way I'd anticipated. I thought it would be me begging him to stay, to love me. Brackish pride welled. It was sour and stagnant because I hurt so much, but it was pride nonetheless that I had settled.

And that I truly believed that it wasn't okay to treat me this way and I wouldn't accept it. Even if it meant losing him. Even if it meant being totally alone.

I wouldn't ask Hollie or Rosa to choose sides. They were April's friends too, and I wasn't going to play the friend break up game where you divvy up the group. I was just going to bow out.

Maybe that's what I needed. A totally new start.

I thought about how empty the house would be without Kieran and maybe it was time for that to go too.

Something like hope surged through me. It was warm and soothing and while it didn't wash away the pain, or fill in the cracks in my heart, it was soft like feathers.

Or maybe it was a padded room. Selling the house was crazy.

Or was it? I'd have more money to invest in *Chubbalicious* and money to live on. I could move to an apartment, get roommates... I spent most of my time in my room anyway. This house hadn't been a real home to me as a child and now that Kieran and I were broken, what was the reason to stay?

I could be shed of everything and really start over.

I could start as the woman I kept saying I wished I was.

Both feet in the frying pan. Why not?

CHAPTER FIFTEEN

I grabbed my laptop and headed to the coffee shop armed with my new sense of adventure and my to do list.

It was time to stop fucking around.

What had I been waiting for anyway?

The easy answer was failure.

Truly, I'd expected to fail in some massive, horrible way. Now it had happened, I'd failed with Kieran and with Brant. I'd lost both of them.

And it wasn't the worst thing in the world. That's not to say I didn't miss both of them, or that maybe some night I'd be sitting by myself in fuzzy slippers, with gelato and watching *P.S. I Love You* and bawling my eyes out. I'm sure I would.

I'd definitely miss watching the stars from the roof of The Rooster and I'd miss Saturdays with Kieran, coffees with the girls, and the way Brant made me feel... I'd miss it all and it hurt that it was all gone.

But I was still here. I still had my dreams and I'd come to the realization that nothing was going to stop me from shooting for those stars I watched so often.

I wasn't afraid to fail anymore.

Even though that lesson came with a lot of pain, it was a gift. I could see that even now.

I bought a mocha and scanned the shop for an empty table. I saw Ryan sitting in the corner and he waved me over.

I lowered myself to the chair and propped my laptop open. "Hey, what's up?"

"Trying to write this paper. Been procrastinating."

I peered around the edge of his tablet and saw a picture of a guy wearing nothing but a jock strap. "I can see why."

He blushed. "It's a calendar I'm working on for the football team fundraiser."

"And who is that?" He was hot, to be sure.

"Fain."

"That's his first name?"

"James Dean Fain."

"Oh Christ, even his name is hot." I looked back and forth from Ryan to the picture. "You like him?"

"Like is kind of a tame word. Obsessed is more like. If he'd just let me see his damn tattoo…"

"You couldn't just, you know, ask to see it?"

Ryan raised a brow. "His standard response to anything is 'fuck you' so I rather imagine that's what he'd say if I asked to see it. And it's on his back. It's like a phoenix wrapping its wings around some kind of brand. I just need to see it."

"Well, if you get any pictures, let me know."

"You're really easy to talk to, Claire."

"Yeah, I get that a lot." I laughed and tried not to feel a hollow echo because that's exactly what Kieran had said to me the day we met.

"Ryan Wells. Who knew?" A petite girl leaned on his shoulder and he snapped the tablet cover closed.

"Who knew what?"

"That you're a chubby chaser. I couldn't figure out why you wouldn't go out with me, but now I know." She looked up at me. "No offense. You're BBW hot all the way."

I arched a brow. "Yeah, none taken."

I was surprised that I meant it. I didn't care what she thought of me and I *was* chubby. Why should the truth be an insult?

"No, Bex. It's not because I'm a 'chubby chaser', it's because you're a bitch."

She took his barb in stride. "Hmm. I guess there is that." She grabbed a chair and pulled it up to the table. "I'm Rebecca, by the way. Only this tool calls me Bex."

"I kind of like it." I shrugged. "It fits you."

She narrowed her eyes. "I can't tell if that's an insult or not."

"No offense," I added with a smirk.

Bex grinned. "Fair enough. I like you. What's your name?"

Ryan interrupted. "This is Claire Howard."

"Oh! The *Chubbalicious* girl." She turned toward me. "You need to put that on a shirt. Pink, black lettering."

"*Chubbalicious* girl?"

She nodded, serious. "I'd wear it."

"But you're not…"

"So?" She grabbed my hand like we were fast friends. "You have to tell me where you got the guys."

"What guys?"

"In the shoot. I saw a couple pictures."

Jealousy surged, but I tamped it down with ruthless precision. I'd decided not to feel that anymore, so I just wasn't going to. I was done. "Actually, they all work at The Rooster."

"The strip club?" Her voice pitched higher.

I nodded. "Yeah."

"So, which one of them are you fucking?" She didn't even bother to try and keep her voice down. I liked how brassy and forward she was. She seemed to mock everyone equally.

"None."

She lifted a brow in a universally recognized motion of calling bullshit.

"Now. None now." I grinned.

"What happened?" Ryan asked. "The big guy?"

I felt on display, but they didn't seem to be asking because there was any malice.

"Come on, I told you my dark secret," Ryan prodded.

"Wait, you have secrets? Why am I just now hearing this?" Bex demanded.

"That's why they're secrets, blondie."

"Fine." She wrinkled her nose. "So, what happened? The tall one looks like a cheater. Is that what happened?"

"Kind of. He was my roommate and—" I proceeded to spill the whole sordid tale. I only kind of knew Ryan, and I'd just met Bex. It was crazy that I was spilling my guts so readily, but it was cathartic. It was like vomiting with the flu. You knew it was going to suck, it tasted bad coming up, maybe even burned, but after it was out, you felt better.

Bex's eyes kept getting wider. She choked on her coffee when I got to the part where I'd slept with Brant and Kieran at the same time.

"You're my hero." She nodded.

I laughed. "Yeah, not so much."

"No, really. Do you not realize what you've done?"

"Screwed up my life?"

"You're living in the fire, not watching it burn to nothing."

"Bex here is afraid she's going to miss something, so she does everything. And everyone."

"Shut up." She sniffed.

"Do you deny it?" he asked.

"I wasn't trying to deny it. I just told you to shut up."

From the look on her face, I suddenly felt like I needed to tuck her under my wing like a mama bird. "Hey, nothing wrong with taking what you want."

"Thanks for saying so. I've been called a slut more than once."

"Of course you have. You're a woman who is comfortable in her own sexuality. That necessarily means you must be labeled, categorized, and filed away for everyone's safety."

That felt profound to me. I'd been guilty of it too, of doing it to myself, my friends—I thought of Brant. I'd thought somehow he couldn't possibly make me happy because he was shorter than me.

But really, happiness? That was my choice. Being with him felt good. I hadn't really given him a chance, I'd just kept pining for Kieran.

I'd even labeled myself fat.

Chubbalicious. That was a label too, literally and figuratively, and I needed to make it a good one.

"You look like someone just turned on a light you didn't know was off," Bex said.

"Something like that."

"So, show me what you have of this website so far."

"No peeking." I wasn't quite that enlightened. All I had were a couple pictures, I wasn't ready for the layout and I sure as hell wasn't going to use those pics of me.

"Come on, I'm dying to see what you do with them," Ryan nudged.

"I'll let you both see a mock up. When it's ready. And not before."

Bex crossed her arms over her chest. "Fine. So back to earlier discussion, what are you going to do about your living situation? Are you really going to sell the house?"

I was terrified to sell the house, so that was probably the right thing to do. I couldn't keep doing the same things over and over again and expecting the outcome to be different.

"Yes, I think I am."

"I could use a roommate," Bex said. "It's kind of lonely."

"Says you with your penthouse view." Ryan rolled his eyes.

"I don't think I can afford penthouse rent."

Bex shrugged. "I'd really just like the company. Daddy's dime."

I didn't know her. This was crazy. Absolutely crazy. But I wouldn't have to deal with Kieran while he tried to find somewhere new to live, I wouldn't have to deal with seeing April or whoever else he wanted to bring home in the interim.

It would be a clean break.

"When can I come see it?"

"Now? Come on, Ryan. Drive us," Bex ordered.

"Bossy much?" He put his things away.

"Oh, you like it. If I wasn't here to give you a healthy dose of crap, who would?"

"Why would you think dosing fecal matter is healthy?" Ryan curled his lip.

"This is why we don't date." She rolled her eyes.

"I thought it was because I never said yes?"

"Whatever." She waved her hand and I followed her outside to Ryan's car.

My stomach twisted up in knots. Was I really going to do this? I hadn't committed to anything. I could still say no.

But I knew I was going to say yes with that certain surety that you have when you see a cop and know he's going to give you a ticket. You see it coming, but it's too late to put on the brakes.

Although, I guess that's not the best analogy because I don't want to put on the brakes. I want to have an adventure. I want to have a new me. A me who is finally comfortable in her skin.

I'd held on to that house with both hands because I wasn't really holding on to the house, I was holding on to my mother. It was time to let all of that go. How could I have any adventures, how could I see a new path for my life if I was anchored there?

It was kismet that just as I'd decided I wanted to do this that an opportunity presented itself. There would always be reasons why I shouldn't do something, so I was going to jump.

Unless of course the whole penthouse thing was a joke and she really lived in a crack alley.

As it turned out, she lived down on the Plaza, and it was indeed a penthouse. While I was looking around the interior, I couldn't believe my good luck.

"Are you kidding me? You'd just… let me live here?"

"Sure." She shrugged. "Why not?"

"I…yes." I nodded. "Yes."

"Yeah? Great! When do you want to move in?"

"Uh, two weeks?" I could give Kieran a month to find somewhere else to live. And if I was honest with myself, which I'd try to do more of lately, it would be so much easier for my heart to forget him if I didn't have to see him every day. Or reminders of him.

I guess it was a little scorched earth, but why not? I'd always held so tightly to everything before. I could just let go and it would be so much better for all of us.

My phone buzzed in my bag. It was a text from Rosa: *WTF?*

Yeah, I guess that about summed it up. I guess April was trying to play the friend break up game I'd already said I wasn't doing. I didn't know what to say.

As I was staring at it, she texted again: *Stop staring at your phone and call me.*

I laughed. "Can you give me a sec? I need to take this."

"Sure," Bex said.

I wandered back to the bedroom with the glorious view that was going to be mine. Then I dialed. "Hey."

"So, what the actual fuck is going on? Kieran is moving in with Gavin of all the fucking people. Really? That's just… I can't…April isn't talking to Gavin or Kieran. Or me."

"I didn't want it to be like this."

"What did she do?"

"Maybe it wasn't her. Maybe it was me."

"Whatever. Of course it was her."

"She slept with Kieran."

"I thought that was a been there, done that, got the t-shirt kind of thing?"

"Yeah. Well, we'd decided to—" What had we decided? "Things took a different turn between Kieran and I."

"A wrong turn?"

"Definitely a wrong turn."

"At least tell me the sex was good."

"It was *very* good."

"Better than Brant?"

The question startled me, slapped me in the face like a bucket of ice. "Actually, no."

"Now that is news. How did Brant take it?"

"Well, we decided to be friends. Kieran, on the other hand, says he can't be just friends with me and I told him to move out."

"He's a fucking asshole and so is April. She just wanted what you had. It didn't have anything to do with wanting anything from Kieran. She was just jealous."

"Isn't she your friend?"

Rosa snorted. "No, she's one of those women who just becomes part of the group, but you're really okay without her. She never had anything nice to say. She was fun to drink with and when I'm feeling mean-girl, she's a good time. But if push came to shove, I wouldn't trust her. Now I see that I'm right not to."

I swallowed and decided to bite the bullet and tell her what I'd decided about the house. "I'm selling the house."

"Good."

"Really?"

"What, did you expect me to tell you not to? No way. You'll have more money to live on while *Chubbalicious* takes off. And it will take off, I know it will."

I could fucking cry. I couldn't believe I'd been so willing to let this relationship go just to get away from April. Rosa believed in me. More importantly, she embodied everything I wanted for *Chubbalicious*. She believed in herself.

"I think I love you."

"Bitch, you better." She laughed.

"So what's happening with you and Gavin?"

"Nothing. He was a good time, but I don't want to date him. I think he and April would actually be very good together."

"Was he a dick?"

"Not exactly. He's ready to be forty."

"What does that mean?" I snorted.

"He wants the yard, the dog, the fucking Volvo and he wants it now. I'm twenty-two. I want to backpack across Europe, I want to take classes just to take them. I want to quit my job just because I fucking can and not worry about my 401K or what kind of roses to send to the bosses wife. I want to write a book, I want to do everything."

"That makes sense. There are some things more important than money."

"So if you sell the house, are you moving to crack central or Volvo land?" she asked.

"Beamer land, actually. Ryan's friend is looking for a roommate and the rent is unbeatable." Couldn't go wrong with free.

"Look at you, getting all fancy."

I looked out onto the carefully planned "outside living area" and I realized I could watch the stars by the pool, swim in the glow of the downtown lights.

"You can come be fancy with me. I'm moving in two weeks."

"Does Kieran know you're selling the house?"

"No, and I don't want to tell him either."

"Okay. I won't tell anyone if you don't want me to."

"How's Hollie?"

"April is so pissed at her too. She's been spending all of her time with Austin."

"Good for her. He's really nice." I was happy for her.

"I'll catch her up on everything when she falls back to earth. I think they've decided to move in together too."

"That's fast." I hadn't expected that. Especially not with Austin's daughter.

"Insta-family." I could hear the shrug in Rosa's voice. "But they're stupid for each other, so I'm not going to poo-poo it."

I laughed. "I love how you can say fuck and still legitimately use the term 'poo-poo' in a sentence."

"That's just how I roll."

"I'm at the new digs right now, so I should probably go. They're waiting on me. You're going to like my new roomie, I think."

"I bring you a housewarming pressie."

"Dinner party by the pool."

"That's all you had to say."

"Thanks, Rosa."

"Anytime. Catch you soon."

I hung up and looked around my new kingdom, feeling like maybe I'd finally taken a right turn.

FAT

CHAPTER SIXTEEN

When I got home, Kieran was gone.

It was as if he'd never been there—at least as far as physical traces of him. He didn't leave anything in his bathroom, no stray cake of soap, no towel hanging over the shower. His room was empty and barren. The bed he'd slept on was there, but it had been there when he moved in. There were no sheets, just the bare mattress perched on the rails.

Even the kitchen… his coffee cup was gone.

Seeing only one cup turned upside down next to the coffee maker, that was what did it. That was what drove it home.

It started as a tickle in my nose, like a bug squirming up toward my brain. My eyes watered, but I couldn't breathe. It was like I was drowning in this wave of loss. I curled up on the bare mattress and bawled.

I'd never sleep in this bed with him again, I'd never curl up against him on the couch to binge watch some series, but even as I sobbed, I realized we'd probably never do those things again together anyway. The us that did those things was dead and gone.

I splayed my hand over the mattress. He'd slept here, but I thought of all the other women who'd been on this bed before me. I wasn't special. If he'd been notching his bedpost to count his numbers, this thing would have been on toothpicks they'd have been whittled down so far.

What the hell did it even matter?

I was disgusted with myself for feeling all this pain. I mourned him like he was dead. He would still be here if I wanted him to be, and I didn't.

I decided to give myself another hour. An hour to lay here, an hour to miss him, an hour to mourn all that could have been. Then I was done with it. I managed a few shaky breaths and set the alarm on my phone.

No more tears fell, but I let myself miss him. I remembered how his arms felt around me, the way he smelled, the way he touched me, and then it went sour again. So I turned my thoughts to what it was like before we'd become more to each other. It occurred to me again that all of his cock of the walk attitude was just posturing, just like me. That made me hurt for him. If I could've taken that away from him, I would have. If I'd seen it sooner, I'd have known that our demons were too similar to ever play together nicely.

As I lay there, I found myself missing Brant, too. I wanted to call him and tell him about my decision to sell the house. I wanted to talk to him about *Chubbalicious*. I wanted to talk to him about the quality of life of flea larvae in Guam—I just wanted to hear his voice.

My fingers closed around my phone, and he'd indicated I could call him, but if he really was ready to talk to me, wouldn't he have sent a text, called, smoke signals, something?

I thought about how hard he'd pursued me, and how I'd rushed into sex with him too. If I hadn't slept with either of them, I wondered where I'd be. Certainly not where I was, and I'd have never known what it was like to have two insanely hot men who wanted me. If I hadn't experienced proof of it with all of my senses for myself, I never would have believed it.

When the alarm went off, I swiped to turn it off with a shaking finger. I knew that it wouldn't be so easy to turn off missing either of them, and I didn't suppose I had to. I wasn't in charge of that, but I'd allowed myself the grief. At least for Kieran, so I dried my eyes and grabbed my laptop again.

Going through the pictures that Ryan had sent me were as sharp a blade as any, but this was for *Chubbalicious*. I was going all in, like I should have from day one. Before I could change my mind, before I could pick myself apart with tweezers and my mother's mocking voice, I chose the picture of me leaned across Austin, Brant, and Kieran as the landing page.

Above our heads it read: I am Chubbalicous.

I plugged the other pictures into the corresponding item pages and descriptions. I worked until everything was done and ready. All that was left was to hit publish and *Chubbalicious* would sink or swim, just like me. In a few days, I'd fling both of us out into the ether and see where we landed.

The knot in my belly had unraveled itself and now it was more excitement than fear.

I found I wanted to tell Brant about this as well. We'd planned to celebrate when I was done. A nighttime picnic with champagne and stars. Not being with him wouldn't stop me from celebrating, but he'd just come to be such a big part of my life in such a short time.

Being around him wasn't like being around Kieran. Whereas Kieran was intensity and fire, Brant was more like a stone. Not that he didn't feel things, I knew he felt them deeply, but he was steadier, solid.

I closed the laptop and wandered around the house, trying not to overanalyze everything.

But my mistakes and failures surrounded me. Kieran's empty room was an accusation. So were the holes drilled into the side of the fridge from when my mother had put a lock on the appliance to keep me from eating when she said I wasn't allowed. I'd never gotten the cabinet fixed from the last time her last boyfriend had hit her. She'd grabbed onto it and pulled the door loose as she'd fallen.

She'd hit her head and never woke up.

Was it any wonder I'd never thought I could do or be anything while I still lived here? The place was full of bad energy.

Only it hadn't been all bad. I'd used to pretend the picnic table in the backyard was a carriage, and I spent hours dressing up and pretending I was living in an Eloisa James book.

It was on the front porch I'd had my first kiss.

And it had been in my bedroom that I realized I was worth more than what life had offered me thus far. It was there when I started walking the walk, believing what I'd been telling myself all these years.

Although it had been in that bedroom I'd lost so much, too. It was tempting to say I'd lost everything, but I hadn't. Not really. I'd found me.

I wandered out to the mailbox and among the various flotsam of bills and junk mail, I found a cream envelope, heavy paper. It was addressed to me in a lovely, flowing script.

Peeling the envelope open carefully, I saw it was a graduation announcement for Brant Edward Bowman. There was a handwritten note enclosed asking if I'd come.

I was thrilled and proud of Brant for working so hard. Of course I'd go. Except I saw that graduation day was the day I'd planned to launch *Chubbalicious*.

After everything that Brant had done for me, I could go to his graduation. The launch didn't need anything from me at this point but to hit the publish button. Advertising was already in place.

What was more, I wanted to be at his graduation.

I walked back up on to the porch, and suddenly, the idea of walking back into that house was just too much. It was like this heavy, oppressive shadow that wrapped strong hands around my throat and squeezed.

The place was just too haunted for me now and I knew I'd made the right decision to move.

CHAPTER SEVENTEEN

Launch day dawned bright and beautiful a week later, the sun streaming through the giant window in my new bedroom. I stretched lazily and my door creaked open, allowing the scents of coffee, almond meal waffles and bacon to waft inside.

"I'm ready to hit the button!" Bex said as pushed through the door. I was happy to see that Rosa was behind her.

"Move over, incoming." Rosa flopped on the bed with me.

"So, I know breakfast in bed is supposed to be fun, but you guys are going to get crumbs in my blanket."

"You sound like Gavin. Maybe you should go out with him," Rosa teased.

"I don't want to go out with anyone," I said. "I'm just going to date myself for a while."

Bex snickered. "Is it still yourself if it's purple and plastic?" She waggled her perfectly waxed eyebrows.

"Shut up. At least I don't have to worry about how it's feeling and it's certainly not going to cheat on me."

"You got that right." Bex pulled the laptop onto the bed and then nudged it at me. "Come on. It's time."

I pulled up the admin portal to the website. Everything was in place. All I had to do was click "publish" and *Chubbalicious* would be born into the world.

Fear and hope tangled together like sticky, spiky vines in my gut. I looked back and forth between the women on my bed. There was nothing left for me to do but jump—fling myself out into oblivion.

"What if it fails?" I whispered.

"It'll never have the chance to succeed or fail if you never push the button."

I thought about Kieran and how I'd had this same conversation with myself about being with him. What if it didn't work? Would I rather be filled with some burning, burgeoning hope and longing for something I thought I couldn't have or would I rather reach for it and know what it's like to hold it in my hand?

Kieran hadn't worked out so well.

But there was more to life than one relationship. There was more to everything than one failure.

So what if I failed? So what? I'd try again. I wasn't going to let anything stop me.

I pushed the button and I waited.

I don't know what I expected, maybe a slow burn. At best, I'd hoped for one or two orders a day, not this.

The site crashed in the first thirty minutes, but not before I'd sold out of all of my stock. The sheer amount of traffic was too much for the servers.

My mouth fell open. "Did that just happen?"

"I think it did. I told you, it was that picture." Rosa grinned and pointed at the screen.

"That was a hot picture. I was hoping you'd have my size because if your clothes will net me guys like that…" Bex grinned.

"That shoot was so hot." Rosa nodded.

"I guess I need to call the supplier and let them know. What if this was just a fluke?" I mean, this couldn't have happened to me. Not like this. I didn't just become a success within thirty minutes of launching the site. Did I?

I didn't know if it was okay to be so happy. Part of me wondered if the second I surrendered to the joy, some kind of bomb would drop and take it all away.

But that was old me talking, that was me who didn't know to expect better.

"Of course it wasn't a fluke. You're officially a successful entrepreneur." Bex handed me a mimosa.

We clinked glasses together and celebrated my success.

"So, are you going to call Brant or Dick—Kieran to take you out?" Rosa asked, not looking at me.

"Neither."

Rosa eyed me.

"Well, I can't say that I don't want to share this news with them both. They each helped me get here. You and Hollie, too. But Kieran is the one who said he didn't want to be friends."

"Could you really have just gone back to the ways things were before? You don't think that would've been a slow death in itself?" Bex asked quietly.

"Maybe. And maybe one day, we'll see each other and we'll say hi. Or…" I didn't want to think about what that would be like. I didn't know if it would be bittersweet or just bitter.

I suddenly had this vision of twenty years later seeing him in a corner store getting bread and milk and I wave, and he waves, there are lines around his eyes making him that much more devastating. And me… I couldn't see myself. All I could see was that we pass each other with a solemnity and a reverence for what was, and maybe contentment with what is.

I guessed that's the best I could hope for.

"What about Brant?" Rosa prodded.

"You're just not going to leave this alone, are you?"

"No," Rosa said.

"Duh," Bex replied at the same time.

"His graduation is today. I'm going to go."

"Oh really?" Bex smirked.

"He sent me an invitation. It's not like that."

"Why the hell not?" Rosa demanded.

"Because, I told you. We both need to heal and I'm not ready to worry about a relationship with anyone but myself. I'm just getting to know me." That was true. I was just getting to know the me I wanted to be and it was hard work to get there.

"Riding Brant like a carnival attraction will in no way detract from your vision quest." Rosa snorted.

"Maybe. Maybe not. He's got his own stuff too, you know. He was really patient while I figured out what I wanted, but I know I hurt him."

"So say you're sorry." Bex shrugged.

They just weren't getting it. I couldn't expect someone to love me until I could love myself. I didn't have anything to give back. I cared about Brant, but was I in love with him?

No.

Could I be? It wasn't out of the realm of possibility it could happen, but I was still healing from Kieran, and most importantly from that voice in my head that told me I was never pretty enough, smart enough, or thin enough.

I had to tell myself every day that I didn't have to be any of those things, that myself was good enough.

"So why are you going to his graduation?" Rosa eyed me.

Okay, so maybe I did want to see him. Maybe I did want to feel what it was like when he looked at me like I was some kind of goddess. Yes, I wanted that, but I wasn't going to play with his feelings to get it. I wasn't going to test him.

I wasn't going to be Kieran.

"He was a good friend, even when it hurt him to be so. I want to do the same for him. I'm proud of him. He worked hard to get here."

"Speaking of working, do you know that he quit The Rooster?" Rosa said while inspecting her nails, as if this wasn't huge news.

"When? Why didn't you tell me?"

"I kind of thought you guys would hash this all out. You know you belong with him," Rosa said.

"And to think, that once upon a time, I was sure he couldn't be anything like prince charming because he's so much shorter than me. I guess that would be like him saying I couldn't be his princess because of how fat I am." I sighed. "You know what? I believed that part too."

"Shut up with that," Bex said.

"No, really. You don't know what it's like. You're thin, petite even." I shook my head. "You don't know what it's like to wear a label."

"Oh, you think? Want to walk a mile in my Louboutins?" Bex bit her lip. "I'm not fat, but I am a slut. Or that's what they call me."

I turned my head sharply. "Really? Why?"

"Because I'm a slut, obviously."

I knew it was meant to be light, but there was such pain behind her words.

"Tell us," Rosa encouraged.

"I don't do anything a man wouldn't." The outgoing Bex was suddenly shy and withdrawn. "I sleep with who I like, when I like. I like sex. So I have it."

"There's nothing wrong with enjoying your body and good experiences. There's nothing wrong with sharing it with who you choose. It sounds like those other assholes have the problem, not you." Once, I might have wished to have her problems instead of mine. The whole world seemed much easier to navigate if I was thin, if I was beautiful. Only, I was starting to make peace with my demons. I wouldn't want to have to start all over.

"My last long term lover said I was a sex addict." She shrugged.

"There are worse things to be addicted to." Rosa took her hand. "I think we're all a little fucked up one way or another. Fuck them and their labels. We don't need them. Just like Claire did with *Chubbalicious*, we define ourselves."

"Yeah, I like that, Rosa."

"The sun has to shine on a dog's ass some time, right?" Rosa winked at me and I nudged her shoulder lightly with a grin.

"So what are you wearing to Mr. Bowman's graduation?" Bex changed the subject.

Pain still lingered behind her eyes, but I wasn't going to push her for more details. I was sure that in time, they'd come. I hope she knew I was there to talk if she needed me. I just went with the flow of conversation then.

"I have no idea."

"What about that cute dress that looked like a mechanic's shirt?" Rosa asked.

"That's probably too casual."

"Would you kill me if I say the cherries?"

I'd been wearing that dress the night we went on the boat tour, the night that things changed between us. "No, I wouldn't kill you, but Brant might have some other memories with that dress."

My face flamed.

"Oh really?" Rosa laughed. "Well, I think it's the woman in the dress that he has the memories with. He didn't make out with the dress."

"That's true. What about the lavender one with the yellow flowers?"

"I thought you weren't dressing to impress?" Bex teased me.

"Well, I'm a fashion entrepreneur, right? I should look the part." What was I doing? Maybe I should just stay home. I wasn't ready to leap back in to anything and neither was he.

"Eat your breakfast." Bex pushed a plate at me.

Under old circumstances, I wouldn't have eaten. As if that would suddenly make me skinny. The oldest habits were the hardest to break. I recited a familiar litany.

It's okay to nourish your body. It's okay to eat. It's okay to enjoy your food.

Only this time, I believed it—I knew it to be true.

I ate the waffle, and I didn't feel guilty or ashamed.

FAT

CHAPTER EIGHTEEN

I kept checking the orders that had come through *Chubbalicious*, just to make sure.

This was really my life.

Success shouldn't have tasted so strange, but it did.

Brant's graduation ceremony was at two so I had plenty of time to psych myself out, but I was determined not to.

This was the new me.

And it was just Brant. Just my friend.

Just the man who once wanted to be my lover, who'd started me on this journey.

As I put on the matching lavender lace bra and panty set, I looked in the mirror. I used to avoid them, but I was determined to look at myself and find something to like about what I saw.

There were stretch marks. Rolls. My belly hung down like a pouch. My body looked like I'd had children, but I hadn't. My hips were rounded, my breasts were full. I wasn't going to let myself choose my breasts as the thing to like, that was the easiest choice. Good breasts were good breasts, it wasn't hard to like breasts.

What was hard to like were the stretch marks, the angry red slashes down my belly. The dimpling on my thighs. The apron of fat of my abdomen.

I pushed my hands down my belly to my thighs. I forced myself to look at it. I liked the contrast of the lavender lace against my pale skin, but that was easy to like too.

No, I was determined to like something unlikable.

My belly. I would find something that made it worthwhile.

I turned this way and that, forcing that reel of negative talk and insults in my head to be quiet. I rubbed it up and down, like a smooth marble Buddha statue. There was a time when only rich women had a body like this, a time when men made statues to honor this kind of shape.

Even though that time wasn't now, I would find a way to honor it myself.

I realized how soft my skin was, like silk. It was substantial, but supple. I wrapped my arms around my middle and there was something nurturing about not just my curves, but even my girth, my width. It was warm. It was safe. It was where I'd offered nurturing to those I loved. It was part and parcel of me.

You are lovable. I looked in the mirror and for the first time, I didn't want to break it so I didn't have to see myself. It was okay to be me. It was okay to be in this body. *You are beautiful.*

I believed it. I really, finally, honestly believed it.

I sank to the floor and I cried.

But they weren't tears of grief or sadness, I guess it was more of an exorcism. I released all the bad that was just hanging out in my skull, ready to infect me with doubt at a moment's notice.

FAT

The crying would make my face puffy, but I didn't care. I let the emotion roll through me, over me, until I could look at myself again.

When I could finally finish dressing, my fingers were clumsy on the buttons. They didn't feel like my fingers because they were so light, like hollow wood. I hadn't realized how much everything had weighed me down, not just my heart, my everything. Knots unraveled in my shoulders, it was easy to hold my head high, my back straight. I wasn't worried about sucking in my belly, or shrinking into the smallest space possible.

After fixing my hair, my makeup and stockings, I looked in the mirror again.

"Hello, you." I said out loud, then satisfied with myself, I drove to the ceremony.

I expected to feel uncomfortable, on display, but I didn't. Not even when there wasn't anywhere for me to sit. I stood in the back and watched Brant get his degree.

Our eyes met, and he nodded to me from the stage and I smiled.

It was so strange how fast life could change. I thought about where I'd been a month ago and where I was now. It was like a different universe.

I wandered from the auditorium to the banquet hall and waited. I debated leaving before we had a chance to talk. Even though he invited me, he hadn't made any other contact.

But he deserved to know how he changed me—how he helped me change myself.

The graduates milled in with their families, but Brant wasn't with anyone. Only himself. He beelined for me.

"Thank you so much for coming." It could have been any nicety uttered from any tongue that afternoon, but it sounded like a benediction coming from Brant. He pulled me into a quick hug, just long enough to smell his cologne and remember how good his arms felt.

Suddenly, I was so glad I'd decided to be brave. "Of course. I know how hard you've worked for this. You should be so proud of yourself."

"I am." He nodded. "I didn't think you'd be here."

"Why not? You asked me to."

He shrugged and looked away. "I quit the club."

"Rosa just told me."

"It served its purpose."

A lot like he and Kieran had. They'd been catalysts of sorts—both of them. "I really wanted to tell you something."

"Yeah?" He looked up, his expression unreadable.

"First, I'm proud of you for chasing your dreams. I think it's amazing that you did this all on your own, no matter what it took. Second, I wanted to tell you that you changed me. In a good way. You didn't just tell me I was a certain thing, you showed me. I don't know if I can ever thank you for that."

He was silent for a long time. When he finally spoke, he said, "How did the launch go?"

"It was…surreal. I sold out in a half an hour."

The unreadable, solemn expression bloomed into a smile. "That's great, Claire. I never doubted your success for a second." Silence reigned again, an icy queen. "How's Kieran?"

I bit my lip. "I don't know."

"That bastard."

"No, it's okay. Really. We talked about it." If you could call what happened talking about it. "And we realized it wasn't going to work. I mean, we hadn't even had one day as a couple before he was fucking someone else. Kieran and I, we're all ashes and dust."

"Surely the friendship is worth saving."

"He didn't want to."

"I'm sorry. This is my fault. It just… I thought you needed to get him out of your system. Or he had to get you out of his."

"Yeah, well, I guess we both did with no half measures." I sighed. "But we don't have to talk about Kieran. I'm here to celebrate your day. To be your friend the way you were mine. You deserve that."

He had gone quiet again.

"Hey, you know, what happened? I hope you're not sorry for that. It was painful, but it was a useful kind of pain. You might even say transformative. I'm not sorry it happened. I mean, part of me wishes that I hadn't said yes to Kieran joining us, but then I'd have wondered. I'd have kept doubting myself."

"Now you don't doubt yourself?" he asked, sounding curious.

"Of course I do." I laughed. "But the difference is that when I talk myself through it, I believe what I say." I shrugged.

"I'm still sorry he treated you the way he did."

"He has his own demons. I guess we all do," I said thinking of Bex.

"You're right about that." He took my hand. "I miss you."

"I miss you too. More than you know." My stupid nose prickled again. I was not going to cry. I'd cried enough in the last month to last me forever. I wasn't that girl, the one who always had tears in her beer.

"Are you sure you don't want Kieran?"

"I'm sure."

"Maybe we can start over, Claire. I'd like to call you sometime."

I laughed. "I'd like you to call me. Hell, let's get crazy. You could even text."

"That might be too rich for my blood." He winked.

"Okay. How about tonight we celebrate like we planned. Midnight picnic, champagne under the stars to celebrate *Chubbalicious* and your graduation."

"You don't think that might be a little too familiar too soon?"

I considered him for a moment. There was no doubt he made my body sing, but that's not what I was after. "No, I don't. See, I want you to be my friend first. Like you offered before. Midnight picnics are my favorite things."

"What if I can't help but get fresh?"

"No, I know you." And I realized that while I may not know everything about Brant Edward Bowman, I knew the important things.

"All the mystery is gone already," he teased.

"Mystery is overrated. Intimacy is kind of nice."

"Kinda. If you're into that." He wrapped his arm around my waist. "So, you want to get out of here?"

"What about the reception?"

"Fuck it. You're the person I wanted here and you came. That's all I needed."

"Okay, it's a long time until picnic time. What do you want to do?"

"How about we get some supplies for our picnic and take some long drives down some unknown country roads until we find a place we like?"

"Yeah, that sounds rather perfect."

As I walked with him out to his car, I knew I was going to get my happily ever after. I didn't know if it was going to be with Brant, but I had the rest of my life with a version of myself I was proud to be.

As it turned out, being fat wasn't the worst thing I could be. I didn't have to change my outside to get my happy ending. I had to change my insides.

One of my favorite romance writers says that happy ever after is a journey not a destination.

I think she's right.

FAT

ABOUT THE AUTHOR

Saranna De Wylde has always been fascinated by things better left in the dark. She wrote her first story after watching The Exorcist at a slumber party. Since then, she's published horror, romance and narrative nonfiction. Like all writers, Saranna has held a variety of jobs, from operations supervisor for an airline, to an assistant for a call girl, to a corrections officer. But like Hemingway said, "Once writing has become your major vice and greatest pleasure, only death can stop it." So she traded in her cuffs for a full-time keyboard. She loves to hear from her readers.

Keep up with releases, events and access to special content by signing up the Saranna DeWylde newsletter here:

http://eepurl.com/LOYTn

www.facebook.com/SarannaDeWylde

www.twitter.com/SarannaDeWylde

www.sarannadewylde.com

FAT

Made in the USA
San Bernardino, CA
13 August 2014